Barney Hoskyns, who lives  critic. His books include *Pri* *Montgomery Clift,* and *Acros* *and America.* This is his first

the lonely planet boy

a pop romance

BARNEY HOSKYNS

Library of Congress Catalog Card Number: 95-68388

A complete catalogue record for this book can be obtained
from the British Library on request

The right of Barney Hoskyns to be identified as the author
of this work has been asserted by him in accordance with the
Copyright, Designs and Patents Act 1988

First published in 1995 by
Serpent's Tail, 4 Blackstock Mews, London N4, and
180 Varick Street, 10th floor, New York, NY 10014

Set in 10pt Galliard by CentraCet Ltd, Cambridge
Printed in Great Britain by Cox & Wyman Ltd, Reading, Berks.

We do not want to see a person on the stage, no, no, no. We want to see a performance, and the poison is the essence of the performer.

Nico to the young Iggy Pop

1

September 1973

Kip Wilson came comparatively late to pop.

Friends had already been into Bowie and Bolan for a year when he attached himself to the little gaggle of Glam Rockers at his prep school. But it was only with the move to Dunstanwood College that he began to live for records, posters, facts about bands.

The week he arrived in darkest Worcestershire, he knew instinctively that it was no longer expedient to like Marc Bolan. Bowie possibly, but not his beloved elfin prince. It hurt to have to hide the treasured copy of *Bolan Boogie*, but sacrifices had to be made if one didn't wish to become a total laughing stock. To attain even a shred of credibility, a quantum jump was now required: a leap into the uncharted waters – the tobographic oceans – of Progressive Rock. In the dormitories of Dunstanwood it was hard to avoid copies of *Tarkus* or *Fragile*.

Kip wondered how he'd possibly be able to afford all these albums. But then he discovered the school noticeboard, with its endless lists of 'Albums For Sale'.

Cream – Goodbye (average nick) £1-50 ono
Groundhogs – Split (good nick) £1-70 ono

Caravan – If I Could Do It All Over Again (fair) £1-20 ono
Land Of Grey And Pink (good) £1-70 ono
Peter Bardens – Same (fair nick) 75p ono
Floyd – Atom Heart Mother (one scratch) £1 ono
Ummagumma (fair) £2 ono
Wishbone Ash – Pilgrimage (excellent nick) £2 ono
Hawkwind – Dore Mefaso Latido (good nick) £1-60 ono
Stones – Ya-Yas (average nick) £1-50 ono
Ten Years After – SSSSH (one scratch) £1 ono

See J. Bowles, Arkwright, 5E

He would gaze at such lists for minutes at a time, mentally computing the kudos which might accrue to him were he to purchase, say, Justin Bowles's fair-condition copy of *Peter Bardens*. But then he had to ask himself just why Justin Bowles wanted to sell *Peter Bardens* in the first place, and for so risible a sum.

He soon obtained his answer. Whilst on wakeup duty in his third week at Dunstanwood, he noticed an impressive-looking record collection in Chris Carter's study. Quickly inspecting the spines before Carter began to stir, he noted the distinct absence of albums by Yes or Focus or Uriah Heep, and the preponderance instead of albums by 'Stone-ground', 'Moby Grape' and 'Quicksilver Messenger Service'.

'What you looking at?', yawned Chris Carter, a shape stirring beneath bedclothes.

'Sorry, I was just checking out your albums . . .'

'You into West Coast bands?'

'Erm . . .'

Two minutes later, Kip emerged clutching copies of the Grateful Dead's *American Beauty* and Country Joe & the Fish's *Electric Music For The Mind And Body*. Chris Carter had told him there was nothing quite like listening to Barry Melton on *Electric Music* while you were tripping, and Kip had grinned nervously.

It wasn't long before the boy was pinning up his own lists of 'Albums For Sale', hoping to offload enough Prog Rock to finance the purchase of *Live Dead* and *After Bathing At Baxter's*. While Bruce Frith and Tim 'Scummy' Mackinnon listened incessantly to Black Sabbath and Rory Gallagher, Kip was busy discovering The New Riders of the Purple Sage.

It must be said that Kip's consumption of rock and roll was rather more obsessive than that of Bruce Frith or Scummy Mackinnon. They liked rock music, but they didn't compile endless lists of All-Time Great Guitar Solos or attempt sketches of Gibson Les Pauls complete with full sunburst finish. The names 'Glasgow Apollo' and 'Leicester De Montfort Hall' did not carry the mythical resonance for them that they did for Kip.

During the summer holiday of 1974, Kip grew his hair as long as he could before his mother protested. Sheila Wilson, who taught history at the local grammar school, retained the liberal views of her Cambridge days but said enough was enough once Kip's hair had reached his slender shoulders. Like many mothers of adolescent boys, she was perplexed by her son's moodiness, and by the long periods he spent in his bedroom. It's hard to say whether she would have been more relieved, or less, had she realised that what kept him to himself for so many hours was less the guilty pleasure of masturbation than the frenetic and all-consuming business of list making: 'Albums To Buy', 'Best Albums of All Time', 'Top Ten Guitarists'.

Kip's father, a professor of medieval architecture at Exeter University, was less concerned about his son. Michael Wilson was a crabby, fusty sort of man who ignored his family and scanned papers through a faintly absurd pair of pince-nez. How Sheila managed to feel fondness for him after twenty years of marriage was a mystery to most people who knew them. But feel it she did, and often in the face of scorn from her own children.

Kip had an older sister, Gemma, who was studying for Oxbridge. She'd been an indulgent playmate until her discovery of older boys, but now she ignored Kip, joining forces with him only when a suitable moment arose to complain to their mother about Dad. To compound matters, she hated rock music and was constantly ordering Kip to 'turn that fucking noise down' on the ancient mono record player in his bedroom.

By the summer of 1975, Kip had befriended Mark Oliver, the only other pupil at Dunstanwood who took rock music as seriously as Kip did. Mark Oliver knew every last thing there was to know about the Beatles, which was enough to make him a soulmate. Kip himself had moved on from West Coast rock to what he grandly termed 'classic pop', a development which made him even more laughable in the eyes of Bruce Frith and Scummy Mackinnon.

That summer, while Bruce and Scummy traipsed off to Knebworth to see 'the Floyd', Kip sat in his bedroom compiling his definitive '100 Greatest Singles Ever Made', except that it gradually grew to two hundred, by which time it included more than a few records he'd never even heard. When it was finished, he sent the list to Mark Oliver, whose family was holidaying in the Scilly Isles. A letter came back almost immediately, howling with incredulity. 'You can't be *serious* putting "Eleanor Rigby" no higher than 34,' his friend wrote, and then: 'Even the staunchest Motown fan wouldn't put "The Tracks of My Tears" at No. 3!' Sometimes Kip would take these protests under consideration and make minor adjustments to his table; more often he would simply return fire, mocking Mark's own Beatles-dominated lists.

Eventually, they were able to compromise on a Top 20 that read as follows:

1 = Strawberry Fields Forever/The Beatles
Good Vibrations/The Beach Boys

3 = I Heard It Through The Grapevine/Marvin Gaye
You've Lost That Loving Feelin'/The Righteous Brothers

5 = My Generation/The Who
Satisfaction/The Rolling Stones

7 Like A Rolling Stone/Bob Dylan

8 Respect/Aretha Franklin

9 The Tracks Of My Tears/Smokey Robinson & The Miracles

10 = Honky Tonk Women/The Rolling Stones
Mr. Tambourine Man/The Byrds

12 Be My Baby/The Ronettes

13 Eleanor Rigby/The Beatles

14 = God Only Knows/The Beach Boys
Dancing In The Street/Martha Reeves & The Vandellas

16 Summer In The City/ The Lovin' Spoonful

17 Reach Out, I'll Be There/The Four Tops

18 = You Really Got Me/The Kinks
My Girl/The Temptations

20 = River Deep, Mountain High/Ike & Tina Turner

All of this made it hard to concentrate on *Emma* and *Heart Of Darkness*. Listening to his English teacher Keith Glatt expounding the themes of 'rebirth and renewal' in *The Waste Land* (or was it *The Tempest*?) was difficult when he couldn't get the Shangri-Las' 'Past, Present, and Future' out of his head. One evening, the ageing pederast who served as housemaster of Arkwright called Kip into his study to ask him what he intended to do with his life. 'Be a rock star, sir,' Kip had replied, only to receive what the man quaintly termed 'a clip around the ear'.

In the early summer of 1976, Mark bought two tickets to see the Rolling Stones at Earl's Court in London. On the train from Worcester the two friends drank cider and bickered about *Sgt. Pepper's Lonely Hearts Club Band*.

'You're telling me *Sgt. Pepper*'s overrated,' said Mark.

'It's a pretentious load of wank,' said Kip. 'The whole Beatles *oeuvre* isn't worth ten seconds of "River Deep, Mountain High". . . .'

'Oh, be serious . . .' He swigged angrily on the bottle of Dry Blackthorn. 'There's no point in having a serious conversation with you.'

Basking in a faint sense of victory, Kip attempted to re-extend the hand of friendship by inserting David Bowie's *Station To Station* into the cheap portable tape recorder that hung over his shoulder. Mark accepted the gesture of reconciliation, smiling as the familiar locomotive intro sounded tinnily through the machine's little speaker.

'From station to station, Worcester to Paddington,' he grinned.

The Stones were shambolic, but Kip was mesmerised. Keith Richards was at death's door and Charlie Watts barely kept time, but Mick Jagger was more grotesquely glamorous than Kip could ever have imagined. As he watched the marble white body flouncing about the stage, pop history flashed before him: the Railway Tavern and *Ready Steady Go!*, Altamont and Anita Pallenberg. Mark was smiling beside him, but Kip felt the chill of awe.

As they piled out into the hot summer night, an ugly youth handed them a flyer for an upcoming gig by 'The Sex Pistols'. Whoever the fuck they were.

2

For Kip, as for so many awkward provincial middle-class boys, punk changed everything.

Shortly after returning to Dunstanwood in that baking hot summer, Kip and Mark made the acquaintance of the Hon. Dominic Nashe, an epicene creature whose peculiar sexual habits – flashing in front of elderly matrons, most notoriously – had almost resulted in his expulsion from the school. It was Nashe who accosted them one afternoon on the school's playing fields, demanding to know if it was true that they'd been to see the Stones.

'Why?' asked Mark.

'So that I should know mine enemies!' replied Nashe pompously.

'What *are* you talking about?' said Mark.

'I am talking about the war,' said Nashe.

'And which war would that be?'

It was Dominic Nashe's cue to unleash a short tirade on the subject of 'punk rock', from its origins in the Velvets and the Stooges to its consummation in the Ramones. 'It's death to the Stones,' he concluded. 'Death to the whole lot of them!'

'Are you quite sure about this?' asked Kip.

That night, he and Mark ascended the creaking staircase that led to Dominic Nashe's study. Stepping carefully over his large collection of porn magazines, they sat on the rather soiled bed and looked around at the posters of Iggy Pop and the New York Dolls which bedecked his walls. Over the course of the next two hours, the pervy aristo gave them a crash course in punk, from Lenny Kaye's *Nuggets* compilation through the Stooges' *Funhouse* to an imported copy of Patti Smith's *Horses*. For his *pièce de résistance*, he unleashed *The Ramones*.

Kip listened in stunned silence to the violent sounds issuing from Dominic's speakers. Watching Nashe whirl about the room like a stricken fighter plane as Iggy Pop howled through 'Loose' and the MC5 pummelled their way through 'The Human Being Lawnmower', he wondered whether he could take this music on board. The savage minimalism of the Ramones was even more jolting: were these deadpan drongos for real or just some cartoon novelty?

The jury was still out when Kip and Mark said goodnight to Dominic, their ears ringing.

'What did you think?' asked Mark as they came down the stairs.

'I have seen the future of rock and roll,' said Kip. 'Not sure if I like it.'

A few weeks later, Kip was confronted by Scummy Mackinnon. 'I hear you've been hanging around with Dominic Nashe,' he said.

'What if I have?' said Kip.

'I hope you'll be very happy together.'

'Not as happy as you and Bruce, surely.'

'What d'you guys do, then, dress up in Nazi uniforms and go to punk gigs?'

'Well, we got a bit tired of wearing cheesecloth shirts and singing along to *Desperado*.'

'You wouldn't know good music if it bit you on the bum,' said Scummy.

In the riotous punk summer of Jubilee year, Kip and Mark went to America together. In New York, their soundtrack was Television's *Marquee Moon*: glistening, crystalline guitars in a cramped rehearsal room. Walking down Broadway with 'Venus De Milo' in his head, Kip asked Mark what he was going to do after university.

'I'm not sure,' he said.

'No, really.'

Mark looked flustered. He knew that in the end he'd do what his parents wanted him to do, become a lawyer or an accountant.

'What are *you* gonna do?' he said finally.

'Form a band?'

'Yeah? What sort of music?'

'Stooges, that kind of thing.'

'Iggy Wilson.'

'Something like that.'

In Los Angeles, they checked into the Fairview Motel on north Cahuenga. Unbeknownst to them, the place was home to numerous junkies, prostitutes and con men. Mark wanted to leave, but Kip couldn't afford anything better. Mark's misgivings were borne out when Kip was naive enough to let T-Man, a stringbean ne'er-do-well from Baltimore, watch TV while they went out for a hamburger. On returning, they found their belongings strewn across the room and their travellers' cheques gone.

In San Francisco they parted company, Kip retracing his Greyhound journey through the flat expanse of the midwest while Mark travelled back down to LA along the coast. By the following summer, the friendship was all but over. Mark gave up buying *NME* and knuckled down to A levels. Kip sat alone in his study listening to *Suicide, Kill City, Talking Heads '77*. To make matters worse, Dominic Nashe was finally banished from Dunstanwood after flashing a fellow pupil's mother.

Kip's two A levels, low grades in English and history, were enough to get him into an undistinguished north London polytechnic. In the autumn of 1979, he moved his record collection into a crumbling terraced house off the Holloway Road, where he was obliged to cohabit with three other students. To his irritation, one of them, a brick-shithouse Geordie named Steve Batterbee, insisted on constantly playing records by Madness and the Specials – records whose upbeat rhythms clashed horribly with Kip's own latest aural passion.

Joy Division's *Unknown Pleasures* really came into its own after Julie Flanagan broke Kip's heart. Julie stood five feet five in heels, with dark hair and piercing blue eyes that Kip would happily have drowned in. She'd fled Dublin for London, one of eight siblings busy dispersing themselves around the globe. He saw her on his very first day at the Poly, her eyes flashing lust across the canteen. For a second they connected with Kip's and he felt his stomach turning over. She had the most perfect bow of a mouth.

Two days later, Kip's gaze once again locked with Julie's. He thought how another boy might have walked over to her and said: 'You a fresher?' Sipping his coffee, he dared to look at her again. Again he fleetingly caught her eye. And then suddenly a tall blond boy was seating himself at her side, pecking her on the cheek. Three days into term and she already had a boyfriend.

At home, Kip masturbated. He pictured Julie's breasts flat under him, the blue eyes closed and the mouth open.

Downstairs, Steve Batterbee cued up the Madness album. To the muffled sound of 'Night Boat to Cairo', Kip came on his stomach.

A week later, Julie Flanagan happened to sit down at his table. He felt himself shiver with excitement. Her black hair was tucked under a cap, and she had dark lipstick on. As she brought a forkful of quiche up to her mouth, she looked over to Kip and said 'Hi'.

'Hi,' said Kip.

'Bit of a shithole, this place,' she said in a husky brogue.

'Totally.'

'I'm Julie.'

'Kip,' he returned.

There was a moment of silence in which he almost choked on a piece of pie. He rescued himself by coughing out the question, 'Are you from Dublin?'

'Yes, for me sins,' she said.

'Why d'you say that?'

'Fuckin' hate the place,' she said. 'Almost as much as I hate me family.'

'Oh dear.'

'Where are *you* from?'

'Near Exeter.'

'OK,' she said, giving him a smile that could just have been construed as flirtatious.

'What are you studying?' asked Kip.

'French and Spanish. You?'

'English.'

Kip worried that at any moment the blond boy would appear. 'Where are you living?' he asked.

'This cesspit in Crouch End.'

'D'you like music?'

'It's all right.'

'D'you wanna see a gig sometime? Or a movie?'

'Sure,' she said.

A week went by before he could pin her down to a date. On the appointed evening, they met at the students' bar and took the tube down to King's Cross. He told her the double bill of *Gun Crazy* and *The Big Combo* came highly recommended by *Time Out*, 'but we don't have to stay for both if you don't want'. She was wearing a black leather jacket and a short green skirt.

Kip sat next to her in a state of permanent sexual excitement. To his relief she thought *Gun Crazy* was 'pretty cool', but they were both hungry and agreed to skip the second film. Over curries, Julie talked about her drunken dad and junkie brother. 'You think you've got drug problems here, you should come to Dublin,' she said.

'D'you do drugs yourself?'

'Me? I tell you, when you've an older brother who's constantly overdosing and gettin' thrown in jail it doesn't look very appealing.'

'No, I suppose not.'

After Kip had escorted Julie back to the door of her Crouch End cesspit, she turned to him and said: 'I suppose you'll be wantin' to shag the ass off me.' He scarcely had time to think of a reply before she'd grabbed the back of his neck and pulled him towards her mouth.

In her bedroom they undressed fast and clambered under the duvet. Kip fought to stop himself grinding into her, sliding down to kiss her small breasts. Julie arched back, pushing his head down to her sex. After some minutes she let out a long groan of relief and stroked his hair. Bursting, he pulled himself back up and steered himself between her legs. He tried to delay the moment of ejaculation by replaying a particularly grim scene from *The Texas Chainsaw Massacre* in his head, but when she stuck a finger in the crack of his ass he spurted into her, burying his sweating face in her neck. 'Good boy,' she purred.

Lying in the stoned afterglow of sex, Kip thought he must be in love. What he didn't know was that Julie Flanagan wasn't interested in love or in anything approximating to it. She'd had enough men in her life, and poor Kip wasn't about to join the ranks of the dipso dad, the scaghead brother and the many other male Flanagans.

Over the succeeding weeks, Julie blew impetuously hot and numbingly cold, finally losing all patience with his hangdog appeals to her pity. 'I don't wanna *be* your soddin' girlfriend,' she shouted outside Dingwall's one night, disappearing into the rain as he leaned against a wall with tears in his eyes.

He took the rejection hard, playing *Unknown Pleasures* repeatedly until Steve Batterbee hammered at the door demanding he desist. Wrapped in an enormous second-hand overcoat, he could be seen floating along the corridors of the Poly like some Edward Gorey phantasm. Had it not been for Stevie, he might have thrown himself off a bridge.

Born and bred in Birkenhead, Stevie had fled to London at the age of seventeen. Two months in bedsitland were all it had taken for him to come out, a revelation his mum affected to find shocking and his dad found 'no surprise whatsofuckinever'. He was in his final year at the Poly.

On Friday nights Stevie earned himself extra cash as a barman in the Students' Union Hall. The Mekons were playing the night Kip slumped against the bar like a wounded bird.

'Whatcha want?' Stevie shouted through the noise of the band and the muffled talk of students.

'Pint of lager?'

Stevie asked him if he was all right.

'Only mildly suicidal tonight,' Kip said.

'What'sa matter?'

'Nothing. Everything.'

'You at the Poly?'

Kip nodded.

'Name's Stevie.'

'Kip.'

Stevie said he had people to serve but he'd come back. Kip turned round to watch the Mekons; more precisely, to see if Julie Flanagan might be in the crowd. If he could just catch her eye . . .

When the Mekons' set was over, Stevie asked Kip if he wanted to smoke a joint. Finishing up, he led Kip into a storeroom.

'You 'ad a bust-up or sommat?' he asked.

'Is it that obvious?'

'Just a guess.' He lit the spliff and took several tokes before passing it to Kip.

'Wharrappen?' asked Stevie.

'It was just this girl, y'know.'

'Yeah?'

'Fucked me over something rotten.'

'So nothing serious. You in love with 'er?'

'No, I fucking hate her.'

'You can't trust women.'

When they'd finished the joint, Stevie said he had to go. 'You wanna shoulder to cry on, call me.' He'd scrawled his number on an empty Marlboro packet.

3

November 1981

The office was its usual dank self. An old XTC poster, peeling at the corners, looked as if it might suddenly drop down on the head of live reviews editor Pamela Motown.

Kip slid in through a side door in his customarily furtive manner. Mild though it still was on the brown streets of Clerkenwell that late autumn day, he persisted in wearing an ancient overcoat, his hennaed hair springing from the collar like a kind of plant.

Kip never quite looked as though he belonged in the offices of *Cover*. He looked bothered, clammy with angst. When he came in on the Central Line of an afternoon, it was always with a dread in his gut, a sense that, in the eyes of *Cover*'s more established scribes, he was nothing but an insignificant whelp. It was his secret dread, indeed, that he would somehow be exposed as an ex-public schoolboy and instantly banned from writing two-hundred word reviews of Barclay James Harvest compilations by an unholy alliance of Stepney soulboys and industrial gloomsters from Leeds.

As it happened, no one paid him much mind either way, since he was merely one of several such freelancers waiting in the wings for any scraps that might be tossed down to them.

Two or three of these abject creatures had already beaten Kip to the desk of Joe Grout, 'Platters' editor of *Cover*, knowing that Thursday afternoon was peak time for the arrival of new albums; knowing too that there was always a chance of worming their way into the weekly editorial meeting.

Kip looked suitably unassuming as he approached Joe Grout in hopes of making off with some albums to review. But Joe was currently on the phone to a press officer at Virgin, saying: 'Lisa, I *swear* I won't run the review early . . .' Kip loathed the feeling of suppliance that came over him as he stood waiting for some tiny acknowledgement of his existence. A thin film of sweat formed on his forehead as he shifted his weight uncertainly from one foot to the other in an effort to look nonchalant.

When Joe Grout had finished persuading Lisa at Virgin that *Cover* wouldn't get her into trouble, he deigned to swivel round in Kip's direction. 'What can I do for you, mate?' he asked, blinking through thick lenses. It was what he generally asked on beholding the rather shabby figure that was Kip Wilson. Kip thought it fairly obvious what Joe Grout could do for him but stammered out his usual reply. 'Just wondered . . . any albums . . .'

Joe stared at Kip without moving, making him squirm in his black brothel creepers. Then he suddenly whirled back round, pulling out the enormous albums drawer with a crash and exclaiming: 'Be my guest!'

Kip felt approximately three feet tall as he made his way round the back of Joe's chair, noting the large flecks of dandruff on the guy's shoulders. In the drawer was the usual collection of unwanted, discarded items: albums by John Miles, Pablo Cruise, *Ten Great Bands From Scunthorpe*. They seemed to stare up at Kip like abandoned children, beseeching him to take them home. As he thumbed ever more frantically towards the end of the pile, he noticed a new album by Alan Vega, erstwhile frontman of the semi-infamous Suicide. Extracting it and waving it in front of Joe Grout's face with a meek look of hope, he received a cursory thumbs down. 'Nick Bliss is doing that,' said Joe.

From the Grout bunker, Kip made his way over to Pamela Motown's desk. Despite her pen name, Pamela Motown was rather lacking in the drollery department. She was also pretty indifferent to pop music. Kip wondered if *Cover* wasn't for her merely a stepping stone to the greater glories of glossy magazines, where her beady eye for vaporous social trends would surely serve her in better stead.

Despite her somewhat haughty air, or because of it, Kip found Pamela Motown intensely attractive. She was petite, with slicked back peroxide-blonde hair and large gold earrings. Today she wore an elegant grey suit, not the sort of thing a *Cover* writer would normally be able to afford but definitely the sort of thing a well-heeled boyfriend might be happy to subsidise. Kip had heard that Pamela's pony-tailed boyfriend Mark managed a club, or a band, or a shop in Soho. Or all three.

'Hi,' he said.

'Hi,' she returned, sucking on a cigarette.

'Anything I could review?'

'Not a lot,' she said, but then smiled faintly: 'Oh, I dare say we can find you *something*.' She proceeded to open a large red diary and locate the forthcoming week's gigs. Kip noticed Material, Bow Wow Wow, James 'Blood' Ulmer, the Birthday Party, but all of them had been assigned to *Cover*'s favoured reviewers.

'See what I mean,' said Pamela.

At the bottom of the page, there were still a few gigs up for grabs: the Barracudas at Queensway Plaza, a band called

Panic at the 100 Club. 'You could always do Panic,' Pamela smirked. 'They're a bunch of Old Etonians with a Glam Rock fixation.' At the very bottom of the list it said: 'Concrete Jungle + Mina, The Cellar, Camden Town.' Concrete Jungle described themselves as 'postmodern funkateers from the futurist ghetto', whatever that meant. Pamela Motown decided it meant enough to merit three hundred words by early Monday morning.

'Thanks, Pamela,' said Kip. He wondered what her real surname was.

Kip saw two rival freelancers hanging shamelessly around outside the cramped office of editor Dez Frippett and hated them for their transparent pushiness. At that moment, Dez himself appeared, returning from a late lunch with the fearsome head of press at Warners. Dez was a survivor from the old days, a man who'd started out as an *NME* stringer long before the advent of the Nick Kents and Charlie Murrays; his dress sense told you he was still living in the mid-seventies, when he'd been jetted around the world in the company of Santana and the Eagles. It was said that he now lived in a pebble-dashed semi-detached in Penge with kids and retrievers, and that he gardened at weekends. To the relief of his wife Marcelle, punk rock had completely passed him by.

'Editorial meeting in five minutes,' he grunted as he entered his office.

There was a general noise of people gathering themselves – the shuffling of paper, the murmur of grievances. Nick Bliss floated in, haranguing everyone around him for the appearance of Echo & the Bunnymen on that week's cover of the paper. Behind him marched Dave Duncan, a stocky Scotsman and *Cover*'s principal black music expert, and Jah Moody, a white Rasta whose brain had fried during an Island Records junket to Jamaica in 1977. Also among the throng of figures making their way towards the office was Ava Cadaver.

Kip had established a bond of sorts with Ava, whose *nom de plume* said as much about her penchant for Gothic camp as did her Morticia Addams get-up. She hailed from New York, where she'd briefly run an East Village club called Trash, and had come to London to spread the gospel of her idol Lux Interior. In her Tufnell Park flat could be found a small shrine to the Vegas-era Elvis Presley, its centrepiece a cheesy 3-D portrait of The King staring beatifically towards rock'n'roll heaven.

Kip liked Ava's sardonic take on 'limeys', delivered in a drawling Manhattan accent. And if he wasn't really her type – she favoured rockabilly ghouls and mutant Elvises – she thought he was cute in his own introverted English way. One inebriated night she'd talked at length about her divorced father, a doctor up in Yonkers, and Kip had responded by talking more guardedly of his own family. Now she sidled up to him and asked if he was coming to the meeting.

'Ooh, I don't think so,' he said.

'Well, why ever not?' she asked in a mock-Southern-belle accent.

'I don't think I really qualify to be in there, do I?'

'Nonsense, you just walk in and *siddown*.'

'If you hold my hand,' he said.

Dez Frippett sat looking benign in the midst of this assembly of highly strung egos. To most of them it was a small miracle that Dez had managed to hang on to power at *Cover* for as long as he had. And yet the extraordinary thing was that, despite being almost completely out of touch with the current music scene, he had a knack for getting the right acts into the paper at the right time. Only his periodic suggestions of retrospectives on Santana or the Eagles could have been said to warrant the abuse frequently meted out to him behind his back.

Kicking off the meeting with an appraisal of the new issue, Dez fielded the criticisms and complaints of his writers with a deft diplomacy. Nick Bliss was still whining about Echo & the Bunnymen, who he said represented everything that was 'wet' about English bands. Talking from behind a pair of Ray-Bans and a cloud of cigarette smoke, he cut a singularly anomalous figure in the assembled company. Dave Duncan, for one, seized on any opportunity to belittle Bliss's outmoded 'rockism'. Bracingly puritanical, Dave attacked anything which could have been construed as corrupt or decayed. He'd recently ascertained that Bliss had taken his pen name from a notoriously junkie-haunted pharmacy in north-west London, and it was just one more reason to lampoon the guy.

Kip didn't really know which side to take in this particular style war. Certainly Nick Bliss was a bit of a joke with his skeletal cheekbones and creaking leather pants – as though one Nick Kent wasn't enough – but then Dave Duncan wasn't a lot more appealing in his loafers and Fred Perry T-shirt. He wondered what other factions there were on the paper.

Joe Grout wanted to know what had happened to half his lead album review, and Dez said he'd complain to the printers. Don Barstow, a grim-looking boy from Bradford, opined that it was high time the Fall were on the cover again. Dave Duncan wanted to interview James Brown, which drew a predictable snort of derision from Nick Bliss. Dez asked Ava how her Birthday Party feature was progressing; she said it was hard getting them together in one place for any length of time. In the corner, meanwhile, sat Jah Moody (née Colin Smalls), staring into space through matted dreadlocks.

Forty-five minutes after the meeting had started, Kip wondered whether anything concrete had actually been decided by these movers and shakers. As people filed out, Ava whispered in his ear: 'Welcome to the cutting edge of guerrilla criticism.' She had been weaned on the gonzo foamings-at-the-mouth of Lester Bangs – had even sat at his feet in the sea of vinyl he called home. For her, these limey prima donnas were 'chickenshit pricks' who spent more time on their expense forms than on their copy.

Kip asked her what she thought of Nick Bliss.

'He's a dick,' she said. 'He was cool a coupl'a years ago, but he's lost it now. I mean, he likes the Psychedelic Furs.'

'That's what I thought,' said Kip, though given the heroes he had in common with Bliss – Iggy, the Dolls, old man Keef – he almost felt guilty saying it. He'd bought more than a few American imports on the strength of a Bliss review. But the guy was plainly fucked, overdosed on junkie cool and ossified punk arrogance. A new order seemed to be dawning, and the Dave Duncans were ushering it in.

Kip was perched on Ava's desk watching Nick totter out of the office when Owen Clark, a gangling anarcho-vegetarian photographer of advancing years, loomed up on them. Dez Frippett had asked Owen to shoot the Birthday Party; Owen wanted to know more about them.

'Psycho junkies from Melbourne,' said Ava. 'Like something out of *Mad Max*.'

'That doesn't really help me,' he said.

'Why don't you come and see them this weekend?' she offered instead. 'Only, don't get too close with the old Nikon. The singer might just smash it over your head.'

Ava only really liked the Birthday Party because of 'Release The Bats', a scorching seven-inch riot of 'voodoobilly' which made even her beloved Cramps sound tame. She'd seen Nick

Cave down at the Batcave and felt mildly intrigued by him. Kip was undecided as to the group's merits but was happy to enlist them in the war against New Romanticism in all its guises. Unfortunately they were playing the same night as his 'postmodern funkateers from the futurist ghetto'.

4

Kip shared his Paddington squat with a motley assortment of human strays. Most of them came and went in quick succession, but Mick and Carla had been in residence since Kip's arrival nine months before. (They never came out). Other inhabitants of the place included Sancho, a product of Holland Park Comprehensive who flogged grass in the Portobello Road, and Ian Treadwell, a struggling thespian then appearing in a fringe production of *The Revenger's Tragedy* in Hammersmith.

Kip's room was a 15' by 9' cell boasting a mattress, a table and chair, and a battered Olympia typewriter. On the floor were records, tapes and books, with clothes strewn across them. A solitary picture hung lop-sidedly on the wall, a poor reproduction of a Pissarro illuminated by a naked lightbulb. Sheila Wilson had once turned up unexpectedly on the doorstep and Kip had had to steer her away from his room with the excuse that he was fumigating it.

Today was Saturday, and a general air of torpor pervaded the squat: the scent of loveless couplings, the pong of puff from Sancho's little lair. Kip woke at midday, too late for hot water. He looked at himself in the shard of mirror that balanced precariously on his table: saw an unshaven twenty-one-year-old boy with a bird's nest of hair and a pale, passable face. He was less sure about his slight white body, with its ribcage showing through.

Kip was teetering on the edge of manhood and didn't care for it. It had been over a year since he'd terminated his studies at the Poly and he was getting nowhere. Voices in his head told him to get a proper job. Mark Oliver worked for an oil corporation; Scummy Mackinnon was in the City. His mother wrote him anxious letters saying he had 'all the time in the world to find a career'; but should 'perhaps start trying a few things out'. It didn't help that Gemma was busy studying at Cambridge.

Kip couldn't think of anything he wanted to do except listen to records. His year at the Poly had given him no more of an appetite for the real world than he'd had at Dunstanwood. Becoming a 'rock journalist' seemed the only possible compromise, except that *Cover* was hardly panning out as a potential career. He'd felt so sure that his Robyn Hitchcock review would lead to greater things, but no one at the office had so much as commented on it – no one besides Ava Cadaver, who didn't especially like Robyn Hitchcock but wanted to cheer up the callow youth she'd seen lurking around Joe Grout's desk.

It was almost dark when Kip finally emerged from his room. Sancho was long gone, and Ian was rehearsing lines in the bathroom. Mick and Carla had their ancient TV on.

He grabbed his overcoat and headed down to the tube. Within twenty minutes he was leaning on the counter at Vinyl Dementia, the Notting Hill store where Stevie worked.

'How's trade?' Kip asked.

'Depends what trade you're talking about, dear.'

'You wanna see a gig tonight?'

'No.'

'Come on.'

'What's in it for me?'

'What d'you mean, what's in it for you?'

'What I said.'

'Nothing.'

'All right.'

Stevie radiated the self-assurance of those who never question the personae they've adopted. Kip was secretive and neurotic, but a smalltown boy who'd come out in the big city had little left to fear – besides the standard prejudice and ignorance, and there were worse enemies. When they were together, Kip wondered if people thought *he* was gay.

'Course they do,' Stevie had said once. 'And they probably think you're the passive one.'

At the Poly, Stevie had given up long hours to hear out Kip's tales of woe over Julie Flanagan. 'You'd be better off coming out the closet like *moi*,' he'd laughed. 'We don't take love so bloody seriously.'

When Stevie had totted up the takings for the day and closed the shop, the two of them made their way to the nearby Man In The Moon, a pub full of boys in zoot suits and girls who wanted to be Grace Jones. 'It's like a photo session for *The Face*,' sneered Kip. Stevie told him to stop being such a puritanical killjoy. 'Look at you in yer overcoat. Anyone'd think you were stitched into that thing.'

He asked Kip how things were going at *Cover*.

'How would I know? It's hard enough getting your foot in the door; but keeping it there is something else altogether.'

'You're doing this gig tonight.'

'One measly live review, for twenty-five quid.'

'They can't ignore yer genius forever.'

Kip described the editorial meeting he'd attended: the out-to-lunch Jah Moody, the feud between Nick Bliss and Dave Duncan.

'How's Miss Cadaver?' asked Stevie.

'She's pretty funny, unlike the other geeks on the paper.'

'Pity she has to dress like the dog's dinner.'

'Least she doesn't wear a zoot suit.'

Stevie said there were some good American imports coming into the shop: the Gun Club, the Meat Puppets, Panther Burns. 'You'd like the Panther Burns record,' he said. 'Alex Chilton's on it.'

Ah, Alex Chilton, the cult hero's cult hero. Kip had gone all the way up to London to buy *Radio City*, the classic album by Chilton's band Big Star. He made Stevie promise to keep a copy of *Behind the Magnolia Curtain* aside.

After a second round of bitter, they decided to make tracks for the Cellar, a notoriously unsavoury dive in Camden.

'Who or what is Mina?' Stevie asked as he inspected his copy of *Time Out*.

Stevie's question was answered as they made their way down the steps that led to the Cellar, for the *chanteuse* in question was at that very moment making her way on to the club's cramped stage.

Kip never forgot his first sight of Mina. With a cigarette lodged between her blood-red lips, she stood with one hand on a hip and the other in the blonde hair that fell around her shoulders. Framed by a polo-necked guitarist and a tall, half-caste double bass player, she could almost have been the Anita Pallenberg of *Performance*.

After her accompanists had run down a loose blues shuffle for half a minute, Mina suddenly seized her microphone and let out a scream that seemed to come all the way up from the pit of her stomach. Kip had never heard anything so scorched or desolate. He stood rooted, struggling for breath. And now the voice was feeling its way through some jazz standard, but without taking any pleasure in the song's sentiments. It was as if Mina was deconstructing the very art of torch singing.

'Deconstructing the very art of torch singing': the line was hastily jotted down on his notepad. Further jottings followed, squiggly lines he knew were running into each other. He wanted to get it all down, feeling the elation a reviewer knows when he's stumbled on something shockingly new. The thrill of thinking he might rush home to write an 'I Have Seen The Future'-style account of this performance made him tingle.

The song ended and another began before the brief flutter of applause could die down. This time it wasn't a torch song at all but a kind of gospel number, delivered in a heaving, orgasmic shudder of a voice. Mina stood with her left arm extended and her eyes half shut, pushing out her thighs as if in the act of copulation. Flanking her, the two sidemen were impassive.

The third song was Jacques Brel's 'Le Plat Pays', prompting the thought that she was covering a lot of bases here. Kip squeezed through the small crowd to see better. There was no doubting her intense presence, yet she seemed almost indifferent to her audience. The voice spat its way through Brel's lyric, until in the last verse she fell with a cry to the floor.

'This is a little hymn to suicide,' Mina prefaced the next song, in an accent that might have been German. 'I learned it from the ghost of Lady Day.' The guitarist sketched out the chords to 'Gloomy Sunday' on his semi-acoustic, and Mina broke into a mock-tragic contralto:

Sunday is gloomy, my hours are slumberless.
Dearest, the shadows I live with are numberless . . .

The way Mina was singing, it was hard to be sure if she was deriding the life the song's heroine wished to depart, or the histrionic lyric itself. But as she launched into the last section of the song, her voice took on a sweetly wistful tone that was more disarming still:

> Dreaming, I was only dreaming,
> I wake and I find you asleep in the deep of my heart,
> Deeeeeeeear . . .

As she held the top note on the last phrase, she leant her head on her bassist's shoulders, fluttering her eyelids like some Walt Disney cherub. The effect was unsettling enough for one beery spectator to yell 'Get 'em off!' and another to shout, simply, 'Get off!'

Mina asked which of the two they would like her to do first.

'Get yer tits out!' came the reply, followed by some uneasy laughter.

To the surprise of almost everyone, she then proceeded to undo the buttons on her shirt, at the same time instructing her backing musicians to supply a suitably sleazy accompaniment. There were rowdy whistles from the crowd, together with tut-tuts and gasps of disbelief. Now the shirt was off, and Mina was standing at the edge of the stage running ring-encrusted fingers over her bra.

'You wanna see my tits, little boy?' she taunted. 'What are you going to do, come up and show me what a big man you are?'

But the little boy in question was noticeably less vocal as Mina went on, the music loping lazily along behind her. This was all too much for the club owner, who now walked on to the stage and ushered her off to the side. Kip thought he detected a faint smile on Mina's face as she hurled her microphone into the crowd.

'Imperious smile of triumph,' he scrawled on his pad.

Stevie was still at the back of the club when Kip rejoined him. 'What did you make of *that*?' he asked Kip.

'I've seen the future of confrontational cabaret and its name is Mina.'

CONCRETE JUNGLE
MINA

Cellar, Camden Town

Descending into this sweaty dungeon on a Saturday night, my hopes weren't high. The place was half empty, the beer had failed to bite, and all things considered I'd rather have been watching the Birthday Party thanks very much. Imagine my surprise, then, when the extraordinary Mina (pronounced Mee-na, I gather) took the stage and proceeded to knock the stuffing out of me.

The first thing that must be said is that Mina is seriously gorgeous, in a disturbing sort of way. Like a young Dietrich, she prowls the stage with arrogant disdain. Her guitarist and bassist aren't a lot more friendly, giving away little behind their blank expressions. The music is . . . well, it's hard to say exactly what Mina does when she gets hold of a microphone. It's a lot of different things, all coming together in her impossible-to-ignore stage persona.

The 'band', if you can call two musicians a band, kicked off the set with a short blues instrumental, after which Mina let loose the most terrifying scream, prior to singing a jazz ballad. Except this was a jazz ballad with a twist – as twisted as it gets, actually. When Mina sings jazz or Jacques Brel, or whatever it is next, you feel she's turning the song inside out, deconstructing the very art of torch singing. She's a cabaret singer from hell.

Mina uses her sexuality to intimidate, to create jarring conflict. Singing a gospel song, she mimed intercourse in a manner which would have had Mary Whitehouse up in arms. It seemed that some of the Stone Age men in the house weren't a lot less troubled, or at least couldn't handle the fact that Mina might eat them up and spit them out for dinner. She was only into her fifth number, 'Gloomy Sunday' (described in a vaguely German accent as 'a leetle hymn to suicide'), when two of these lads turned the Cellar momentarily into a Harrogate working men's club. They told Mina to 'get 'em off'.

Well, to say she rose to the challenge would be an understatement. 'You wanna see my tits, leetle boy?' the avenging ice-blue angel sneered, ordering her guitarists to play a strip-tease motif while she began peeling off her clothes. This confrontational tactic brought the club's owner on to the stage double fast, and the set to a premature close. But by that time we'd seen enough to know that Mina is a new and dangerous force in the hygienic climate of sartorial synth-pop. She strutted off the stage with an imperious smile of triumph on her face.

Forget Concrete Jungle. After the bracing

slap-in-the-face that was Mina, their industrial funk routines and grainy back-projections left me cold. Their music was as grey and soulless as the boiler suits they wore, which might be the point but didn't make them any more appetising. They had a hard core of gloomy-looking fans who appeared to treat them as prophets, but the only thing prophesied here was their own imminent extinction.

Kip Wilson

5

On the Thursday that his Concrete Jungle/Mina review was published, Kip could be seen creeping nervously into the *Cover* office. Clutching the paper in his hands, he retired to an empty desk to inspect his contribution. This was a moment at once eagerly anticipated and deeply dreaded. Worst case scenario was that the review wouldn't have been run at all; more likely, it would simply have been hacked to bits by Pamela Motown or one of the *Cover* subs.

To his amazement, the review was virtually intact. Heart thumping, he re-read it several times.

'This Mina sounds pretty wild,' a languorous American voice said over his shoulder.

'Oh hi, Ava,' he said.

'I can't believe she actually started to strip!'

'It was pretty hard to believe if you were *there*. How were the Birthday Party?'

'Pretty fuckin' wild. Maybe they should get together with Mina.'

At that moment, the gangling form of Owen Clark emerged from the recesses of Dez Frippett's office.

'Recovered from your Nick Cave experience?' asked Ava.

'Just about,' he replied.

Owen Clark looked older than his thirty-seven years: his long hair was almost totally grey and large bags had formed under his eyes. He'd been taking photographs for the pop press for more than fifteen years, having started out as an errand boy for one of Swinging London's less illustrious *paparazzi* before disappearing to live on a commune in 1968. Some of his shots from the sixties were famous, but in music press circles he was more renowned for clinging obstinately to certain vestigial hippie ideals. He'd recently found a new lease of life shooting pictures of the anarchist bands who'd surfaced in the wake of Crass. Despite the scorn of Dave Duncan and others, Dez continued using him as one of *Cover*'s main photographers.

'Owen, you know Kip Wilson,' said Ava.

'Hullo,' said Owen.

'How're your kids?' Ava asked.

'Yeah, they're fine, Ava.'

'How many is it you've got now?'

'Oh well, you know . . .'

It was hard to be sure whether Owen was embarrassed by the number or had actually lost track of his progeny. Ava had heard there were three or four mothers involved.

The office was slowly filling up with writers, most of them leafing through *Cover* to check that their pieces were as brilliant in print as they'd been in typescript. Nick Bliss, for instance, was poring over his Gun Club feature, cursing with irritation every time he spotted a cut or an error. Dave Duncan had satisfied himself that his overview of the career of George Clinton was a masterpiece of socio-musicological analysis and was presently hounding Pamela Motown for his James Brown tickets.

Joe Grout was on the phone to Kelly at RCA.

At the usual appointed hour, Dez Frippett signalled that it

was time for the editorial meeting. For the second week running, Ava led Kip into the editor's office and sat him down by the window. Kip looked out over the darkening streets, afraid again that Dez or Joe or someone would say: 'Sorry, what are *you* doing in here?'

Dez fished a packet of Rothman's out of a drawer and asked for feedback on the new issue.

'I think it's good,' said Don Barstow, whose Cabaret Voltaire feature had provided the cover story.

'I think it's crap,' said Nick Bliss. 'A bunch of sappy Scousers one week, a bunch of dreary Yorkshiremen the next.'

'Our readers happen to like these bands, Nick,' said Dez.

'Which is more than can be said for the Gun Club,' added Dave Duncan.

'Gentlemen, gentlemen,' said Dez.

But there was no stopping Dave Duncan, who'd led the rock-is-dead faction almost from the day he'd joined the paper and wasn't going to back down now. He wanted more black music in *Cover*, more politics, more fashion. If he'd been the paper's editor he would have purged it ruthlessly, junking old farts like Nick Bliss and Jah Moody and Owen Clark. There was nae room for such people in the bright new dawn of soul-cialism. His chief sidekick in this campaign was a po-faced second-generation mod called Malcolm Reeves. Malcolm backed Dave all the way, interjecting remarks such as 'Yeah' and 'I agree' at any available opportunity.

Had Kip been asked where he stood on these vital questions, he'd have been hard pressed to answer. Was rock dead? Were ABC really the way forward or just a bunch of poseurs with too many James Brown records? Kip liked Marvin Gaye as much as the next man, but did that mean sweeping out everything deemed 'rockist' by the likes of Duncan, who'd spent much of 1981 being flown to America to cover the antics of artists on the Ze label.

When the squabbling had died down, Dez wanted to know if anyone had ideas for the Christmas issue of *Cover*. He was met by a stony silence. Jerry Dammers? Sting dressed up as Santa? The Human League?

'You could do a sort of *Christmas Carol* cover, with someone dressed up as Scrooge,' put in Pamela Motown.

'Not a bad idea,' said Dez.

'How about Nick Bliss?' quipped Malcolm Reeves.

'You've got your monkey very well trained today, Dave,' said Nick.

'Fuck off,' said Malcolm.

'Fellas, please,' groaned Dez.

The sparring took a more veiled form for the remainder of the meeting, occasionally piercing the fog of ennui which had settled on everyone. Kip found the whole occasion even more dispiriting than the previous week's gathering.

In the end, it was agreed that they would ask Phil Oakey to dress up as Father Christmas – 'with his dolly birds in reindeer outfits', suggested Nick Bliss to general hissing – and fill out the rest of the issue with the usual lists and end-of-term reports.

Kip was following Ava to her desk when Dez Frippett called him back into his office. For a second it felt like being summoned by a headmaster; a tremor of fear shot through him. 'Come and sit down a second,' said the editor.

It transpired that Dez had read Kip's review and wanted to know more about Mina. 'What would you say to doing a short feature on her/' he asked.

'Great,' said Kip.

'Nothing too heavy or detailed, you know, just six hundred words telling us what she's about.'

'No problem,' said Kip, trying to conceal his excitement.

'Is she signed to anyone?'

'I'm not sure, actually.'

'Well, I'll put someone on to it, see if we can't set something up.'

'Thanks a lot.'

'Do we have a phone number for you, Kip?'

'Erm, not right at the moment.'

'Well, check in with me tomorrow or Monday.'

'Sure.'

Kip walked out of the office on air.

'Cat get the cream or *what*!' said Ava.

'He wants me to write a piece on Mina.'

'Way to go! But be careful – she sounds dangerous.'

'Let's hope so.'

6

Visions of Mina were all that remained after a sleepless night.

At 9.15, Kip heaved himself out of bed and staggered into the kitchen. Sancho was just back from a long night of clubhopping, his eyes bloodshot and his face the texture of parchment. 'How you doin', man?' he asked in a pointless American accent. Kip said he felt like shit.

The kitchen stank. There was crockery in the sink that hadn't been washed in a fortnight. Sancho sat on the table swinging his legs. Kip decided to go out for breakfast. He called Stevie, who said he'd be at Sid's in twenty.

Sid's was the greasy spoon of choice in the area, mainly because it wasn't full of beer-bellied brickies. As he came in, Kip saw Stevie already wedged behind a corner table. He'd cropped his hair and added a second ring to his right earlobe.

'You look ill,' was Stevie's greeting.

'I *am* ill. What the fuck am I going to ask Mina?'

'Ask her about sex.'

'Stevie, I've never done this before.'

'You'll do *fine*. What's the worst that can happen?'

'That I end up feeling a complete prat?'

Sid's son Derek came over to take their orders. Stevie

fancied him and gave him a sort of rolling-eyed leer. Kip decided on a mushroom omelette, to be washed down with Sid's amphetamine-strength coffee.

'First of all,' said Stevie, 'have you checked yer batteries and all that stuff?'

'Yes,' said Kip with a groan.

'Well then, all you need's about twenny daft questions and hey presto, you too can be Paul Morley.'

Kip felt better with food inside him. They finished up and settled Sid's bill. Outside, the sun had come through the clouds and Praed Street didn't look quite so depressing.

Kip took the Central Line to Tottenham Court Road and made his way into Covent Garden. It was here that Mina's manager Rick Stubbs had an office, a dingy set of rooms over a stationer's off Long Acre.

Kip pressed the bell marked 'Spearhead Management' and stood in the street for half a minute. The second time he pressed it the door buzzed and he entered, ascending the staircase with butterflies in his stomach. To his relief, Mina did not appear to have arrived. On red stilettos, Rick's secretary Cindy tottered off to summon her boss, returning to ask if Kip wanted tea or coffee.

Rick Stubbs entered the room mopping his brow with a large handkerchief. His skin was a mottled grey-white and he had bluish bags under his eyes. Kip rose to his feet and felt the clasp of a wet palm.

Now in his late thirties, Stubbs had started out as a scout for EMI, graduating to become an A&R man with Capitol in the seventies. When punk happened he'd switched to management, lucking out with a band who did well in the States. But things went terribly wrong when the band in question left a Pistols-style trail of destruction behind them and were unceremoniously deported. Rick had never quite forgiven them for losing him all his money. Now he was struggling to keep his little operation afloat with the aid of 'the lovely Cindy', as he called her, and a roving dogsbody known simply as 'Spud'.

'Er, *Cover*, right?' he said.

'Right,' said Kip.

'So what sort of piece is this gonna be, eh? Long one, I trust.'

'It'll probably have to be quite short, actually.'

'Hmmm . . .'

'But we'll probably follow up with a longer one.'

Rick slumped on to a black leather armchair and stuck a John Player Special in his mouth. 'How's old Dez doing?' he asked.

'Fine, I think.'

'Dear old Dez.'

'Have you known him a long time?'

'Dez? Yonks, mate. I was dealing with Dez when the Beatles were still at EMI.' It was a lie but it sounded good.

Kip sipped his almost undrinkable chicory coffee.

'By the way,' said Rick. 'Word of advice about the young lady you're about to interview.'

'What's that?'

'A bit moody is our Mina. Tread softly.'

Kip felt his butterflies again. 'In what way, exactly?'

'You know. Don't ask any boring questions. Keep her amused.'

'Right.' He gulped down the rest of his coffee.

Rick left the room and half an hour went by. Kip tried to calm himself down by reading one of the trade magazines on the bamboo coffee table.

At a quarter to twelve there was a buzz and Kip heard Cindy say, 'Oh, hello, Minnie.'

'For fuck's sake, Cindy!' roared Rick from his office. 'How many times do I have to tell you Minnie is not her fucking name!'

'Sorry Rick,' said Cindy, pulling a mock-terrified face for the benefit of Kip. Except that Kip *was* terrified.

The door swung open and there was Mina. Dressed in a full-length leather coat, her eyes masked by sunglasses, she swept straight through reception to Rick's office.

After several minutes of shouting and door slamming, she reappeared, the sunglasses removed. Kip got to his feet and proffered a hand. In heels she seemed to tower over him.

'Are you ze guy from ze paper?' she asked, her voice slightly hoarse.

'Yes, I am,' said Kip.

'I am Mina,' she said. 'Let's go.'

She led the way down the rickety old staircase and out into the street. As they walked towards the Strand, she jammed a cigarette in the corner of her mouth.

'Rick is a good manager,' she said.

He wasn't sure if she was joking, or why she even had said it. Suddenly they were turning a corner and entering a pub called The Goat In Boots.

'What do you drink?' she asked as she walked up to the bar.

'I'll just have a lager, I guess.'

'A lager and a large brandy,' she told the pink-rinsed woman behind the bar.

'Thanks,' said Kip.

When they'd sat down, Kip pulled out his tape recorder and microphone.

'Do you hev to use that thing?'

'I don't have to, but . . .'

'Go ahead and use it, it's OK.'

'Are you sure?'

'Sure,' she said, adding: 'I suppose I should thank you for your review.'

'Oh, that's OK,' said Kip, adjusting the volume level.

'The trouble is, I think maybe you give people the wrong impression of what I am about.'

'I'm sorry?'

'Yes, I think people perhaps will not understand. "A cabaret singer from hell." Hmmm.' She took a large mouthful of brandy and grinned. Kip felt overpowered by her green eyes.

'Well, I'm sorry if I caused offence,' he said.

'Offence, no. Slight, how you say, puzzle?' Another smile.

Just as Kip was opening up his sheet of questions, Mina leant across and snatched it from his hands. She examined it, saying 'boring, boring, boring'. Kip thought his nightmares were coming true. 'Can't you ask me something interesting?'

He swallowed uncomfortably.

'OK,' she said finally. 'This is my story. I woss born in a little town in the Austrian Alps. My father was a sadist. He beat me and my brothers every night. My mother was a very depressed woman. I hate my family, my father beats me and my brother tries to fuck me. I heard stupid folk songs and drinking songs in this town, I didn't like them. I listen to Radio Luxembourg on my radio and I hear the Rolling Stones and the Yardbirds. These I like. When I am twelve I left to go to Vienna. I became a model and also a prostitute. I live with a stupid gangster man from America.

'When I am sixteen, I went to Hamburg and live with a drug dealer. I hear that my father has died and I feel nothing. My brother says I must come and look after my mother, I said fuck you. In Hamburg, a friend of my boyfriend has a nasty little nightclub, like where the Beatles played maybe. He heard me sing in the bath or something, probably looking at me in the, how you say, keyhole? He says, "Do you wanna sing in the club, Mina?" and I said OK. I started learning songs, you know, "Cry Me A River" and "Lush Life", but it's not enough, because I want to sing dangerous songs. You understand me?'

Kip was so flabbergasted by what she was saying he merely nodded. He wondered how much of this was true, or if she was just some crazy girl from Basingstoke living out a bizarre fantasy. He turned off his tape recorder while she went to get another brandy.

'So I ended up in Berlin,' she continued after returning. 'I lose the drug dealer guy and meet this other guy who plays with a band. He is called Manfred. He asks me if I wanna sing with his band, which is like a punk band. I told him I can't sing punk, but he puts me in the band. Once we got the support with Siouxsie and the Banshees in a club, but the drummer, Fritz, he overdosed so we cannot play. What a bunch of jerks, especially Manfred. I got pregnant thanks to that prick.'

She paused to light another cigarette.

'Then last year I come to England. I went to stay with my friend from Hamburg, she is in Bristol. But then I came to London and I met Dave, my bass player. Dave, he doesn't say much but he's OK. He asked me did I wanna sing with him and his friend, I said sure. That's pretty much the story.'

'Can I ask you how many gigs you've done?' asked Kip.

'Maybe ten . . . not many.'

'Have you enjoyed them?'

'Enjoyed? No, I have not enjoyed them. We play in these horrid fucking places.'

'Are you deliberately confrontational?'

'Do I like to confront? No, but if somebody starts to piss me off, you know? Maybe I piss *them* off. For me, it's a matter of – instinct? Is that the word? I am not setting out to attack anybody. It depends on the atmosphere in the place.'

'Have you ever worked in the theatre?'

'Yes, I've worked in theatre. I've been a stripper! No, but really, I was in a theatre group in Berlin when that asshole Manfred ever let me do what I wanted. They talked all the time about Artaud, you know him?'

'Antonin Artaud? I've heard of him.'

'This is a great man.'

'Do you consciously use your sexuality in an aggressive way?' Kip was aware he was very slightly blushing.

'Of course. What is the body? It is just something you use to make a point. When I sing, my whole body becomes like my voice, you understand? My body does whatever my voice says it must do.'

'Were you being sacrilegious during that gospel song you did?'

'What is that?'

'Were you . . . attacking religion in some way?'

'I don't remember. Sometimes I am not conscious of what I'm doing, I just move. If it is sexual, then it's sexual. Why should there not be sex in religion?'

'Well, sure, but . . .'

'But nothing.'

'Um . . . do you think you're shaking up male pre-conceptions?'

'I am not a feminist. Perhaps I shake up my *own* precon . . . ceptions? Men, well, who cares? They are welcome to shout at me. I am used to men shouting at me!'

'Do you think you have a cynical world view?'

'No. Just because I sing, say, a Brecht song does not make me a cynical person. Perhaps you should not try to put these labels on me.' She smiled and threw back the rest of her brandy.

'What do you think of the British music scene?'

'I don't think about it, I am not interested. There is one group I like, but this is a German group, the Deutsche Amerikanische Freundschaft. Do you know their song "Als Wär's Das Letzte Mal"? "Like It Was The Last Time"?

Drück dich an mich,
Gib mir so viel wie du kannst.
Liebe mich mein Liebling,
Als wär's das letzte Mal . . .'

'I have that album,' Kip was pleased to be able to say. 'Tell me, are you working on your own record?'

'Yes.'

'What sort of stuff are you doing on it? Are you doing any original songs?'

'It will be about half original and half . . . not so original!'

'Do you write yourself?'

'I am writing the words, and Dave and Boris write the music.'

'Your guitarist is called Boris?' asked Kip with a slight smile.

'Yes, is that funny?'

'A bit.'

'Well, that is what he is called.'

'Can you tell me anything about the songs?'

'I cannot tell you, except they are all good songs and most of them are about death.'

'Death?'

'Yes, I am very interested in death.'

'Anything specifically?'

'*Everything* specifically!'

Kip was about to ask more when the door opened and in walked a spotty youth in a baseball cap.

'Oh, *mein Gott*,' said Mina. 'The curse of my fucking life.'

Panting like a bedraggled spaniel, Spud – for it was he – spat out his message.

'Rick says . . . you gotta come . . . back to the office . . .'

'All right, I come,' she said, turning back to Kip. 'I'm very sorry, but I hev to go. I hope you got what you need for your article. You call the office if you wanna ask any more boring questions.' She shot him another smile.

The leather coat and the baseball cap disappeared through the door.

FEMME FATALE

Kip Wilson meets Mina, a different kind of torch singer

Pic: Nigel Smart

Mina comes into her manager's office in a full-length leather coat and shades. For a minute you think she must be a Strip-o-Gram, but when she marches across the room and starts abusing the manager in question, you realise this is no part-time dominatrix.

We repair to a nearby watering hole to talk about Jacques Brel, Billie Holiday, and other heroes. Mina is a hot-tempered, frighteningly beautiful singer who has very little time for the bright, jolly world of British pop. She moved here from Berlin (though she was born in Austria) a year or so ago. Since then she's played several gigs with Boris (guitar) and Dave (bass), one of which your humble correspondent was lucky enough to witness a couple of weeks ago.

To say it was the most shocking performance I've seen in ages would be an understatement. Not only can this woman sing in no uncertain terms, with a voice at one moment tenderly sensual and the next utterly blood-curdling, but she has more charisma in her left eyebrow than all Brit girl singers put together. She turns jazz ballads, gospel songs, and cabaret numbers into a pure theatre of attack. When she started to strip during the gig, the Stone Age men in the audience seemed more frightened than excited.

Interviewing Mina is not the easiest job in the world. Throwing back brandies, she dismisses my questions and tells her own story:

'I was born in a little town in Austria. My father beat me and my brother tried to f--k me. My mother was very depressed. I heard stupid folk songs and drinking songs, and I didn't like them. Instead, I listened to the Rolling Stones and the Yardbirds. When I was twelve, I left our town to go to Vienna. I became a model and a prostitute, and then I lived with a gangster from America.'

She goes on in this vein, talking about her father's death and living with drug dealers. She says she first started singing in a club in Hamburg, where a friend 'heard me and asked me if I wanted to sing songs like "Cry Me A River" and "Lush Life"'. But this wasn't enough for Mina. She wanted to sing *dangerous* songs.

Later, when she got to Berlin, she joined a punk band who were due to support Siouxsie and the Banshees when their drummer overdosed. When she came to London, she found allies in Dave and Boris, with whom she has written the songs for her forthcoming album.

So is she deliberately confrontational, I ask.

'Do I like to confront? No, but if somebody starts to piss me off, maybe I piss *them* off. It's a matter of instinct. I'm not setting out to attack anybody, it just depends on the atmosphere.'

Does she want to shake up male preconceptions?

'I am not a feminist. Perhaps I'm shaking up my own preconceptions. Who cares about men? They are welcome to shout at me. I am used to men shouting at me!'

She tells me she's very influenced by the French writer and actor Antonin Artaud, and that she really likes D.A.F.'s *Alles Ist Gut*. She says most of the songs on her album will be about death, a subject which fascinates her.

'Anything specifically?' I ask.

'*Everything* specifically!' she shouts.

7

Thanks to his Mina piece, Kip now found himself being accorded a certain respect by Joe Grout – and even being tacitly acknowledged by Nick Bliss. More gratifying still was the invitation to *Cover*'s Christmas shindig in a club off the Charing Cross Road.

On the night of the party, Kip was finishing an album review in his room when Stevie dropped in on his way home from Vinyl Dementia. 'So the Teutonic siren turned up trumps for you,' he said. 'Told you you'd go far.'

'Well, steady on.'

Stevie asked what the party would be like.

'Don't know, really. Be interesting to see.'

'Your mate Ava be there?'

'I hope so.'

'Wharrabout Mina?'

'Unlikely.'

Stevie sat back on Kip's bed and began rolling a joint.

'Do you want to come?' Kip asked.

'No, ta. Got a date.'

'Yeah?'

'This luscious boy who comes into the shop. Likes dodgy bands but I can overlook that.'

'What's his name?'

'Get this – *Ralph*.'

'Ralph?!'

'Sexy or what?'

'If you say so.'

'Yer just jealous.'

Stevie lit the joint, passing it over to Kip after three tokes. 'You going home for Christmas?' he asked.

'Guess so. You?'

'Me? You've gorra be joking.'

'What about your mum?'

'She's gonna have to come down if she wants to see me.'

'What you going to do on your own?'

'Oh, you know . . .'

'I'd invite you to stay, but . . .'

'But yer folks might get the wrong idea.'

'Well, you just wouldn't like them. Or my sister and her delightful fiancé.'

'Don't worry, kiddo,' said Stevie, taking back the joint. 'I wouldn't wanna intrude on such a cosy occasion.'

At that moment, lured by the drifting odour of the joint, Sancho popped his head round the door. He was wearing an orange kimono.

'Hey guys,' he said. 'Couldn't 'elp catching a whiff of the 'erb. Mind if I, er, partake?'

'I thought you sold this stuff,' Kip said irritably.

'Just finished the stash, actually.'

'You may . . . *partake*,' said Stevie, faintly repulsed by the figure standing before them.

'Champion,' said Sancho, seizing the proffered spliff.

'Any sightings of Mick or Carla lately?' asked Kip.

'Nope,' said Sancho inhaling.

'I sometimes wonder if they haven't just died in there.'

'Nah, they're just out of it, aren't they?'

'Are they?'

'Junkies, mate.'

'You sure?'

'I've *scored* for 'em a coupla times.'

'Where's yer other flatmate?' asked Stevie, who'd been rather taken with Ian Treadwell on his last visit to the squat.

'That poncy git,' said Sancho. 'Struts around all day like Sir Laurence Oliver.'

'Olivier,' said Kip.

'Rather tasty, all the same,' said Stevie.

'What, you a poof or summing?'

'A what?'

''Ere, no offence, mate . . .' Sancho had begun to sound like a newspaper boy in one of the less celebrated Ealing comedies.

'Mr Treadwell regrets he cannot give autographs at the present time,' said Kip. 'This is due to the fact that he is currently auditioning for the role of footman in a Whitehall farce.'

'So what's 'appening tonight, guys?' asked Sancho.

'Your flatmate is guest of honour at the *Cover* party,' said Stevie.

'Yeah?' said Sancho. 'Can you get us in?'

'Not your sort of crowd, I wouldn't have thought,' said Kip.

'Oh, come on.'

'No, really, I can't. You've got to have a special invite.'

'Guess it'll 'ave to be the Fridge again.'

'Go for it, Sancho,' said Kip.

Kip arrived at the party a little after ten. As he edged his way through the sweaty crowd, he saw Dave Duncan and Malcolm Reeves in the DJs' booth, spinning what the former loudly proclaimed to be 'the hottest imports aroond!' The place was crawling with female press officers, all the Kellys and Shelleys under the sun, most of them being hit on by drunken hacks. Kip even noticed the odd pop-star-in-decline, frantically milking the last seconds of his or her celebrity for all the attention it afforded. In a darkened corner, finally, he could just make out Nick Bliss and his anorexic girlfriend in matching leather pants.

Kip searched for Ava Cadaver and found her upstairs with Dez Frippett, who was busy holding court with a group of balding men with names like Ray and Reg and Ron. 'Aha, the new blood!,' said the slightly inebriated editor as Kip approached.

'Hi there,' said Ava, quickly steering Kip away from the table. 'Wondered when you'd show up.'

'I couldn't stay away.'

'You wanna drink?'

'Love one.'

Ava had barely turned towards the bar when Kip caught a sudden glimpse of Julie Flanagan, all of twenty yards away on the arm of a swarthy-looking boy in a leather jacket. He felt his stomach fall through the floor. Either she couldn't see him or she'd already clocked him and was studiously avoiding eye contact.

When Ava returned with two bottles of Beck's, Kip looked as though he'd turned to stone. 'You seen a ghost or something?' she asked.

'Sort of,' he said. 'An old, um, friend.'

'Oh, one of those. You wanna siddown?'

'Yes,' he said, managing somehow to turn away from Julie Flanagan.

'I take it this wasn't a friendship which ended amicably.'

'You could say that.'

'Where is she?'

'Well, she's sort of over there,' he said, straining to see her.

'Next to the guy in the leather jacket?'

'"Next to him" is the understatement of the year.'

'Ouch!'

Dave Duncan had put on a thunderous piece of discofied rock called 'Bustin' Out', prompting Ava to drag Kip on to the dancefloor. The fact that neither of them could dance did not unduly bother Ava, who'd set her mind – for the sheer sozzled hell of it – on taking Kip home with her. As Nona Hendryx's angry voice screamed through the record's raging guitars, Ava flailed away, crucifix banging against her chin. Kip, on the other hand, made only the most rudimentary movements: with one eye out for another agonising glimpse of Julie, and the other making sure no one was watching him, he was really in no fit state to 'strut his stuff'.

After Dave Duncan had segued from 'Bustin' Out' to some more obscure 'floor-filler', Kip told Ava he was going to the bathroom. As he was about to enter the gents', he virtually collided with Julie Flanagan. 'Kip!' she shouted through the music.

'Oh, Julie.' It was all he could manage.

'What're *you* doing here?'

'I write for this paper, actually.'

'You do? Maybe you could do a write-up on my boyfriend's band!'

Kip thought this crassly insensitive, but managed to ask what they were called.

'The Lost Souls,' she said, cupping a hand round his ear. 'They're *really great*!'

'But then you would say that,' he replied.

'You may be right there, Kip,' she laughed.

'So what've *you* been up to?'

'Oh, odd jobs. Nothin' too exciting, that's for sure.'

They were joined at this point by the Lost Soul himself, a rock'n'roll gypsy with black curls and thick earrings. He was taller and broader than Kip.

'Kip, this is Mark,' Julie said. 'Kip writes for *Cover*, Mark! I said he should do a write-up on you!'

'Sounds good to me,' said Mark.

'Well, it's not actually up to me,' said Kip, stifling his hurt.

'We'll get a tape to you, mate,' said Mark. 'Got an album out in a coupla months.'

'Great,' said Kip, vowing to throw the thing straight in the bin.

'So Kip, tell me,' said Julie in a fluting sort of voice. 'You got a girlfriend yet?' It was the ultimate insult.

He wanted to lie but said no.

'Happy huntin'!' she said by way of goodbye.

He watched them continue on their way, her arm hooked into his. He wanted to crawl into the filthiest piss-stained toilet and die.

On the tube up to Tufnell Park, Kip swigged from a can of Kestrel lager while Ava talked about the New York subway. The train stank of beer and saveloys, but Ava said it was a pleasure cruiser compared to the D train.

The first thing Kip saw in Ava's flat was the Elvis shrine. When she hit a switch, neon tubes lit up and illuminated the rapturous face of the bloated god. For a second, Kip thought Ava was about to prostrate herself before him, but she merely bent down to adjust the little arrangement of rhinestones, pill bottles and hamburger cartons which lay under the 3-D portrait.

'How long've you been a practising Elvisist, Ava?'

'Ever since I realised he was the patron saint of Trash,' she said.

'So when did you create this masterpiece?'

'When my mom moved to Florida a few years ago. I used to get a fresh Big Mac for it every day, but now I make do with these plastic Whoppers.'

'Didn't the Big Macs start to smell?'

'I always had the air conditioning up high in my room.'

Kip wanted to keep talking about Elvis in order to avoid the real issue at hand, which was whether or not they were going to sleep together. He drained the last drop of the Kestrel and popped open a can of Special Brew. Ava put the kettle on and rummaged around in a small pile of videos she'd brought from America.

'How do you fancy *The Crazies*?' she asked. 'Or I have *Suspiria*.'

'I don't mind.'

'George Romero is my all-time favourite director, but Dario Argento comes close for sheer baroque intensity and evil.'

'Sounds good,' said Kip.

'You want some coffee to go with that vile stuff?'

'I'm OK, thanks.' In fact, he was close to passing out.

'I don't have any drugs to offer you.'

'No probs. This elixir . . . *suffices*.'

Ava made herself a coffee and sat down beside him. When *Suspiria* started, he felt so smashed he could hardly distinguish the film from the reflection of the Elvis shrine on the TV screen. The final swig of Special Brew produced a loud burp.

The young heroine of the film was just arriving in the Black Forest when Ava reached her hand over to unzip Kip's fly, and a gruesome sequence of events unfolded on the screen. For several minutes she attempted fellatio.

'That one's a goner,' she said eventually.

'Sorry,' said Kip.

After a few more girls had been spectacularly despatched, they retired to Ava's bed, but it was to no avail. Kip lay at her side, relieved that it was over.

'Great English lovers of our time,' she sighed.

'My pleasure,' said Kip.

7

At home that Christmas, Kip kept to himself as much as he could. In his old bedroom, which still had posters of the Clash and the Ramones on its walls, he read Philip K. Dick's *A Scanner Darkly*, periodically emerging to eat a bowl of cereal or watch television. On Christmas Eve, he took a bus into Exeter to buy presents for his family. But he'd barely been in the city ten minutes when he was waylaid by a new record shop, complete with bargain bins. When he finally got home three and a half hours later, he'd managed to find a wicker basket for his mother, a pair of shears for his father, a cushion for Gemma and a cravat for her fiancé Jeremy.

Jeremy Bagshaw was quite the dreariest person Kip had ever met. He studied at Cambridge with Gemma and took every opportunity to ingratiate himself with their parents. To Michael Wilson's credit, he thought Jeremy every bit as boring as Kip did. But then Michael Wilson thought most people boring, as he made patently clear in his blithe disregard for anyone else during yuletide. To Kip, it seemed as though his father only invited the likes of his brother Andrew for Boxing Day lunch in order the more pointedly to ignore them.

In an effort to compensate for her husband's rudeness, Sheila Wilson bustled busily about the house making sure no one experienced a split second of boredom or hunger or discomfort. Occasionally she stuck her long neck and bedraggled head of greying hair into Kip's room, asking if he wanted to join them all for tea or a card game. Kip always said that he did not. Once he was sure there was no one in immediate earshot, moreover, he'd put on the Stooges' 'Loose' or Captain Beefheart's 'Big-Eyed Beans from Venus' and leap around his room playing air guitar.

That Christmas it snowed, which made Sheila bustle about even more than usual. 'It's so snug and cosy,' she liked to say, though it provoked only a peremptory grunt from Michael, who could usually be found slumped in front of the fire reading *Private Eye* or the *New Statesman*. The sight of his father in the sitting room made Kip want to smash the pince-nez which sat on the bridge of his nose. But in such feelings he no longer had an ally in Gemma, who simply ignored her father and channelled her needs into Jeremy Bagshaw. The two lovebirds could frequently be seen holding hands on an old window seat, bringing little gasps of joy out of Sheila as she scuttled past.

'So what've *you* been doing with yourself?' Gemma asked Kip on Christmas Day.

Kip said he'd been doing nothing.

'*Nothing*?' his sister retorted. 'What d'you live on?'

'I sponge off the state, don't I.'

'What, and spend all the money on records, I s'pose.'

'Oh, records and drugs, you know . . .'

'How shocking,' she said with heavy fatigue.

'Hullo, Kip,' said Jeremy, who wore a beige cardigan and brown corduroy trousers.

'Hullo, Jeremy,' said Kip.

'Nice to have a white Christmas.'

'I suppose so.'

'Kip used to love tobogganing. Didn't you, Kip?'

'Did I?'

'So what's happening on the, er, *pop* scene, Kip?' asked Jeremy.

'Oh God, don't ask him that or we'll be here all day,' said Gemma.

'There's nothing happening, Jeremy. Apart from this incredible singer called Mina, who sings Kurt Weill and Jacques Brel songs. As a matter of fact, I interviewed her a few weeks ago.'

'You did what?' said Gemma.

'Interviewed her.'

'What for?'

'For *Cover*.'

'So you *are* doing some work.'

Sheila Wilson came bustling into the room with some logs under her arms. 'Hullo, you lot,' she sang out. 'Any of you want to come for a walk?'

'That sounds lovely, Sheila,' said Jeremy.

'We'll come with you, Mum,' said Gemma.

'Think I'll pass,' said Kip.

'God forbid you should join in for two seconds,' said Gemma.

'"*Join in*"?!!', Kip exclaimed.

'Oh, let's just go,' said Gemma crossly.

When Kip got back to London, he found a letter awaiting him in the squat. It was written in a shaky and childlike scrawl.

Dear Kip Wilson,
        Great little piece on my BIG STAR Mina. Ta! She

wants to say Ta! too. Also, were gonna be recording at
Holy Grail in Archway from next Tuesday and would you
like to come down. Youre realy going to LOVE what
she's doing now. The album is gonna be BRILL. You can
call us on the office number any time.

Rock'n'roll

Rick Stubbs
Spearhead Management

Kip wondered how Mina could entrust her career to such a
boor. Perhaps Stubbs's odious manner was simply a disguise
for his ruthless business acumen.

Three days later, Kip took the tube up to Archway and
trudged through the slushy snow to Holy Grail Studios. As
he entered the darkened building, he was accosted by a
menacing figure in a balaclava and duffle coat. It turned out
to be Spud.

'You lookin' fer Mina?' he asked.

'That's right.'

'Yeah well, she ain't 'ere yet.'

'Right.'

Spud sat himself down and proceeded to roll up some
baccy in a cigarette as thin as a drinking straw. 'You're the
journalist, incha,' he said.

Kip nodded.

'You the geezer what wrote summing about 'er in *Cover*?'

'The very same.'

'Come back fer more, 'ave yer?'

Kip wasn't sure what Spud meant, so let it go. 'Is she
always late?' he asked.

'Yeah.'

'How long has Rick been managing her?'

'Fuck, I dunno. A year?'

'How long have you worked for him?'

'Two years?' He sucked hard on his straw-thin roll-up. 'Fucking cold, innit.'

'Freezing.'

''Ow d'you get into that writing lark anyway?'

'Um, you just pester people till they give you something to write.'

''Oo you interviewed, then?'

'Well, I've only just started, really, so . . . so hardly anyone.' He couldn't quite bring himself to admit that Mina was his only interview to date.

'What d'you reckon to Mina, then?'

'I think she's brilliant.'

'Yeah?'

'Yes.'

'Well, that makes two of yer anyway.'

'Sorry?'

'You'n'*er*!'

'You don't like her?'

'Don't get me wrong, mate, she's a lovely girl. But the music? Come on. Rick's always tellin' 'er she's gotta think big, thing *global*, but she don't listen to no one but 'erself. Oops . . .'

Just in time, Spud had noticed Mina entering the reception area with Rick. Bringing up the rear were Dave Mackaye and Boris Salgado, both carrying their instruments, and a man who turned out to be their producer.

Mina looked particularly striking that morning. She wore a black suit with heavy Doc Martens, and her hair had been cut into a starkly androgynous parting. Dave and Boris, also in black, resembled bodyguards more than musical accompanists, their instrument cases making them look like comic-book gangsters from the roaring twenties. Only Rick Stubbs, in a cheap and ill-fitting raincoat, cut a less than dashing figure in the little procession.

'*Heeeey*,' said Rick as he saw Kip. 'If it isn't Kip Wilson.'

'Hi,' said Kip.

'So glad you could make it. Can't *wait* for you to hear the new stuff.'

'Great,' said Kip, wondering if Mina would say hello.

'Thanks for the piece, man,' said Dave in a gentle Mancunian voice.

'Wasn't it great, boys,' said Rick. 'Gives us something to build on, that's for sure.'

As they walked into Studio A, Kip caught Mina's eye.

'Hello,' she smiled, extending her hand in greeting.

'How are you?' he managed to say.

'I have been better,' she said as she followed Boris into the studio's control room. Once everyone was huddled round the console, an engineer rewound a spool of master tape and played through the previous week's work.

Kip was immediately shocked by the dark, droning electro-pulse which enveloped them. The sound was huge and hypnotic, a Giorgio Moroder-ish dance epic full of swirling synth effects. Through the storm of noise came a gaunt, grave voice:

Midnight winds are landing at the end of time . . .

Boris, noting the vaguely puzzled look on Kip's face, leaned across and said: 'Nico, "Evening Of Light". It's a sort of *reinterpretation*.'

'Who did the programming?' asked Kip.

'I did, actually. With a little help from Clive here.' He indicated Clive Finch, the producer.

The song was building to an almost monstrous climax of shuddering cross-rhythms, with Mina sounding even eerier than the song's original *chanteuse*:

The children are jumping in the evening of light,
The children are jumping in the evening of light

'Brilliant,' said Kip as the track faded. No one else spoke. Mina lit a cigarette.

'Well?' Clive Finch finally asked. He was thirty-five-ish, one of the hot indie producers of the day.

'I want to redo the guitars in the second half,' said Boris.

'I cannot hear myself,' said Mina.

'Tell me something, Clive,' said Rick. 'Can you honestly hear that on Radio 1?'

'No,' said Finch without batting an eyelid. 'Can you?'

'But I thought the whole point . . .'

'There *is* no whole point,' said Boris. 'I mean, how could a Nico song *ever* make a Radio 1 playlist?'

'I met her once, y'know,' said Rick, as though that fact alone entitled him to criticise the track. 'What a sad old bag she is now, eh?'

'No sadder'n you,' said Dave.

'Yeah? Thanks a lot, Dave. At least I don't have syringes jangling about in my bag.'

'No, just little pocket mirrors and rolled-up twenny pound notes.'

'If I do *a little coke* now and then, at least I keep it very quiet. And totally under control.'

'That's not what *we* heard,' said Dave.

'Oh, and what did *you* hear?'

'There's a lady present, Rick.'

''Scuse me, guys,' interjected Clive Finch. 'Are we working or what?'

'Sorry, Clive,' said Rick, who knew he'd been lucky to get Finch for the session.

Throughout this little exchange, Mina had sat blowing smoke rings in to the corner of the room, a sullen expression on her face. Suddenly she rose to her feet.

'I am going home,' she said. 'Finish the track without me.'

And turning on her heel she was gone.

SINGLES: REVIEWED BY DON BARSTOW

SINGLE OF THE WEEK
Mina: Evening of Light (Tarantula 12")

A mesmerising maelstrom of a dance opus.

This curious new trio with the iconic blonde singer have taken the closing track on Nico's classic *Marble Index* and turned it into a massive vortex of sound that spins you senseless and twists you into a trance. The song builds slowly to a furious climax, with Mina intoning her forbear's words with a spooky detachment. As a dance record it works brilliantly: 'The children are jumping in the evening of light', indeed. But it's more than a dance record. It's eight minutes of intoxicating abandon, a rollercoaster ride of riches, a journey to 'the end of time'. Synths scream, guitars erupt like little volcanoes, and still the hypnotic beat goes on.

I don't know where Mina and her henchmen are going next, but I like the opening sortie. Invest in them now.

8

Kip read Don Barstow's review of 'Evening of Light' with a twinge of irritation. 'Typical,' he moaned to Stevie. 'It's like a stringer on a provincial paper breaking a story and some Fleet Street slob taking all the credit.'

But Kip couldn't complain about the work he was getting now. In addition to the usual dodgy live reviews – bands like Artery and Experiments With Ice – he covered American imports acquired from Vinyl Dementia, commencing with a two-in-one review of Rank & File and Our Favorite Band! and following up with features on Romeo Void and Sonic Youth. In March, he reviewed the Jam, earning himself a certain notoriety around the *Cover* office for calling them 'the ultimate post-punk Sacred Cow'. In the squat, his typewriter could be heard clattering away at all hours, to the point where Ian Treadwell claimed he couldn't learn his lines properly.

Kip particularly relished any chance to lambast the hygienic, fresh-faced pop of Haircut 100 and their ilk. 'Haircut 100 are simply a hand-knit Bay City Rollers,' he proclaimed in one gratuitous aside. Nor was he a lot better disposed to ABC, with their glittering suits and plastic Trevor Horn production. It was outright war on the charts, with everyone from Non to the Bush Tetras enlisted as guerrilla opposition.

An ally in this war, of course, was Ava Cadaver, with whom Kip continued to conduct an odd sort of relationship. Ava had forgiven him his lacklustre performance after the Christmas party, but he still flinched at the whole idea of her as a sexual partner. Their dates were as a consequence slightly uncomfortable, however much Kip enjoyed her sense of humour.

When Ava decided to hold a little 'wake' for the recently deceased Lester Bangs, Kip asked if he might invite Stevie. She said that of course he could come, on the condition that he try to locate a copy of Lester's 1979 single 'Let It Blurt'. Along with *Metallic K.O.* and *White Light/ White Heat*, the record would provide the theme music for the evening. Stevie duly managed to 'borrow' 'Let It Blurt' from Vinyl Dementia and turned up in Tufnell Park at the appointed hour to discover that Ava had chosen to give the wake a Gothic ambience, embellishing the Elvis shrine with a selection of candelabra and illuminated skulls.

'What's this?' Stevie muttered to Kip from the side of his mouth. 'Voodoo night down the Tufnell Park Rialto?'

'Try and be nice,' said Kip. He wondered whether the mourners had ever read a word Bangs had written. Half of them seemed to be Cure lookalikes or skeletal Australians Ava had met down at the Batcave.

After an hour had passed, Stevie decided he could take no more. Fuelled by the bottle of Yugoslav Riesling he'd been cradling, he sauntered up to his hostess and demanded to know the relevance of all this Gothic paraphernalia.

'I beg your pardon?' asked Ava, herself well lubricated by this time.

'Well, sorry if I failed to notice sommat, but I never associated Lester Bangs with the Hammer Horror school of rock.'

'What's your point, douchebag?' Two or three tattooed Australians had already rallied to her defence.

'What I'm saying, love, is would Lester Bangs really have gone in for this sort of Batcave crap?'

'Listen, you jumped-up little fruit, you can get the fuck out of here right *now*!!'

'OK, mate,' intervened one well-meaning boy from Brisbane. 'Sounds like you've had a few too many, eh?'

'Fuck it!' raged Ava. 'If this little fag wants a fight I'll give him a fucking fight!'

But the Brisbane boy had taken Kip aside and asked: 'Is he a mate of yours or what, mate?' And when he'd determined that Stevie was indeed Kip's 'mate', he suggested they escort the truculent Scouser off the premises.

Kip needed little persuading of the wisdom of this move, and with the help of the Australian he managed to manoeuvre Stevie out of the flat, all the while imploring Ava's forgiveness. Finally they were in the street, sobered by the cold night air.

To Kip's amazement, Stevie collapsed on to a nearby bench and began howling with laughter.

'Do share the joke,' Kip said tersely.

'Don't you see?!' screamed Stevie. 'That's just what me dad would've done!'

'Which makes it all right.'

'*I* think so,' said Stevie, who began howling again.

'You're an asshole.'

Kip walked down the hill towards Tufnell Park tube, Stevie trailing behind him and singing a medley of songs from his favourite musicals. He finished with his best take on Judy Garland:

> The night is bitter, the stars have lost their glitter
> The winds grow colder, suddenly you're older,
> And all because of the man that got away . . .

Teetering on the edge of a wall, one arm raised skywards, Stevie bellowed the song into the night – to the great amusement of passers-by and the continued embarrassment of Kip Wilson, who promptly disappeared into the tube station.

A week later, by way of making amends to her, Kip took Ava to see five Kenneth Anger films at the Electric Cinema. Afterwards they adjourned to a nearby mews house where her friend Melissa was throwing a party. ('Theme: Black.') This time the Australians were thinner on the ground, Kip recognising in their stead a smattering of London punk celebs-in-decline, along with Nick Bliss and his girlfriend.

Towards midnight, a slight hush fell over the festivities as the great Johnny Thunders staggered into the room. He looked wretched, a pinned Pacino swaddled in leather. His hair was matted and his skin greeny-yellow. Kip remembered the cover of the first Dolls album, with Johnny's semi-erect cock bulging through his leather pants. You couldn't put your arms round a memory, but you could watch his spectral form go through the motions of survival.

As Thunders made his way into the kitchen, proceeding to rifle through various drawers in search of a spoon, Kip couldn't resist taking up a better vantage point. While he did so, Melissa rushed over to the former punk legend with the neurotic concern of a society hostess who has failed to make the correct introductions. 'Johnny!' she almost wailed. But

Thunders merely grunted, grabbing a spoon and seating himself at the kitchen table.

Kip watched Thunders prepare his hit, blackening the underside of the spoon as he heated up a whole teaspoonful of heroin with water and citric acid. After drawing the brown liquid through a piece of cotton wool, he spent an eternity hunting for a vein in his calf, cursing as each attempt to hit blood failed. Finally, 'the little orchid bloomed in the barrel' – at least that was how Kip recalled the standard William Burroughs description – and Thunders pushed the plunger into his leg. Instantly he sank back into his chair, all feeling apparently extinguished. The syringe remained dangling in the air like an arrow in the side of a tree.

Kip turned away with a kind of sick elation in his stomach. Rejoining Ava, he reported what he'd just witnessed.

'Good old Johnny,' she smiled like the seasoned New Yorker she was.

'Beware the evil poppy,' drawled a voice behind them. It turned out to belong to Nick Bliss, who was leaning against the fireplace with a look of immense scorn on his face. Beside him stood Karin, the anorexic girlfriend.

'Well, there you go, Kip,' said Ava. 'A salutary warning from the voice of experience.'

'Ava, anyone'd think you were some sort of evangelist,' said Nick. 'Can't you let the fair youth of our nation fuck up without interfering?'

'Oh, back off, you old serpent.'

y. 'Did you see Thunders in the kitchen?' asked Kip ingenuousl-

'Did I see him?' replied Nick. 'I've seen Johnny banging up in most quarters of the globe. I've even done it *for* him.'

'You're supposed to go, "Oh wow, Nick!"' said Ava.

'But you see, Johnny doesn't talk to me any more,' said Nick. 'Not since my review of *So Alone*.'

'How's *your* drug habit these days?' Ava asked him.

'Mind your own business!' hissed Karin.

'No no no, darling,' said Nick. 'I've absolutely nothing to hide. Let's just say a drop of the green stuff a day keeps the doctors away. Plus the odd, uh, treat now and then.'

'By "the green stuff", I take it you mean methadone,' said Ava.

'You said it, not me.'

'That's what happens to all the old junkies eventually, Kip,' said Ava.

'Hark at her!' said Nick. 'I had no idea a Cramps fan could be so bloody prudish.'

But the conversation ceased suddenly as Thunders himself brushed past them. There was no hint of recognition as his colourless eyes, glazed marbles in the sallow face, briefly locked with Nick Bliss's.

'Dear Johnny,' said Nick as the diminutive figure passed.

There was a further pause as the four of them watched the short leather legs disappear from the room.

'By the way, Kip,' said Nick Bliss. 'Perhaps you should know that your Austrian vixen is not averse to a drop of the hard stuff.'

'I'm sorry?' said Kip.

'Yeah, your friend Mina. Bit of a junkie, I hear.'

MINA
La Ronde (Tarantula)

There were those who thought Mina and her henchmen would not go the full long-playing distance. 'Evening Of Light' was an ambitious one-off, they said, a freak deviation into dance-land. They may now eat their words.

Mina – with Dave Mackaye, Boris Salgado and sundry supporting players – has delivered everything she promised: an extraordinary album about joy and pain, desire and betrayal, fidelity and prostitution, taking its cue from a famous play by her countryman Arthur Schnitzler. This is where we see her moving out from her 'cabaret' base to set her seal on a multitude of new styles.

In Schnitzler's *La Ronde* (filmed in 1950 by the great Max Ophuls), the baseness of lust is revealed through a sequence of affairs that connects the lowest stratum of society with the very highest. In Mina's version, the thread of illicit desire links each song to the next, gaining a cumulative effect and climaxing in the darkest tragedy. Each track presents her as a different character, even (singing in a near-contralto voice) as a man. In 'Ugly', she's a disfigured prostitute, in 'The Death Of Desire' an embittered countess. 'American Friend' turns her into a psychopathic GI, 'Ghost' into a lesbian poetess. Yes, it's pretty ambitious stuff all *ronde* . . .

The album kicks off with 'The Love Market', a typically cynical *chanson* from old Bertie Brecht and Hanns Eisler which serves as the prostitute's theme song. The song's piano motif recurs from time to time through the album, which now continues with the powerful, almost Velvets-style 'Poison Doll'. On this number, Mina is a seductress planting the seed of the disease – a sort of fatal *ennui* – that spreads through the record's subsequent liaisons.

'Poison Doll' feeds immediately into an

astonishing version of Roxy Music's 'Bitter-Sweet', the reading of which takes Ferry's melancholia/chorus-line dichotomy to the limits of kitsch. Where Ferry was a lounge lizard mutating into a goose-stepping Nazi, Mina is a world-weary Dietrich who turns into Wendy O. Williams on heat, screeching over thunderous metal guitars. You'll have to hear 'Carlos', the plaintive swansong of a Brazilian transsexual, to appreciate the full scope of this album. 'American Friend', meanwhile, is reminiscent of the petrified funk of James White & the Blacks. Over Boris Salgado's choppy Telecaster riff, Mina and her three male backing singers intone the terrifying tale of GI Joe, who rapes Carlos in the Bois de Boulogne.

It's GI Joe who continues *la ronde* when he visits the scarred prostitute in 'Ugly', the first track on side two. The title notwithstanding, the song is oddly pretty, with a hypnotic chord sequence that intriguingly underpins the details of their sad copulation. Ugly herself becomes beautiful in 'Ghost', a ballad sung by her dead lesbian lover. Mina has never sung quite as well as she does here, sounding like a cross between Edith Piaf and Marianne Faithfull. Dave Mackaye's double bass playing is no less outstanding, providing a perfect counterpoint to the vocal.

But perhaps the real highlight of the album comes with 'European Nights', a pounding dance *meisterwerk* set to an awesomely robotic rhythm. In this song, Mina manages to conjure an eerie sense of decadent high society, by turns damning and rapturous. The lesbian poetess of the preceding song here recounts mem-

ories of her husband's infidelities, together
with her own seduction by the wealthy countess who becomes her patron. Finally, that same
countess looks back over a wasted life in 'The
Death Of Desire' and prepares to commit
suicide. Here, Mina sounds for all the world
like Billie Holiday in her last broken years. As
this desolate ballad winds down, we again hear
the piano motif from 'The Love Market': *la
ronde* has come full circle.

There are precious few other people out
there in popland who would even attempt such
a 'concept album', let alone succeed in making
it work. With *La Ronde*, Mina has become
something more than a singer; she has become
an artist of astounding force and depth. And in
Mackaye and Salgado, with their unique fusion
of jazz and electronics, she has found the ideal
collaborators to help realise her bracingly
bleak vision of human relations.

Kip Wilson

9

Kip was well aware that his review of *La Ronde* was partly an impersonation – a mimicking, almost – of the lit-critical style of John Oldfield.

No one knew much about Oldfield, a reclusive eccentric who lived in a run-down tower block and rarely showed his face in the *Cover* office. He was said to have studied with Michel Foucault in Paris and to be writing a vast polymathic treatise on art and morality. In his very occasional contributions to *Cover*, he invariably cited several weighty continental names to bolster his arguments for the greatness of the most unlikely artists. It was no surprise, for instance, to find a reference to Kierkegaard or Rainer Maria Rilke in a short paean to Stevie Nicks, or a quotation from Wittgenstein's *Philosophical Investigations* in a review of Donna Summer's *Bad Girls*.

'Very John Oldfield, your review,' said Dez Frippett when Kip came into the office that week. 'Who's this Schnitzel guy, anyway?'

'Um, he was a playwright,' said Kip.

'Any good?'

'I never read the play, but I saw the film.'

'Well look, go easy on the intellectual stuff, eh? One John

Oldfield's quite enough for this paper.' Dez shuffled back into his office, but then almost immediately reappeared and caught Kip before he'd turned the corner.

'Kip,' he said. 'How would you feel about writing a proper feature on Mina?'

'Christ, I'd love to. If you don't feel I've already written enough on her.'

''Sfar as I'm concerned, you're the one who discovered her, so you should have first crack.'

'Well, what can I say?'

'She's starting a tour next week. I'd like you and Owen to go up to Liverpool. I've checked it out with Rick Stubbs and there shouldn't be any problem.'

'He told me you and him go back a long way,' said Kip.

'Who, Rick? Is that what he said?'

'Something like that.'

'Yeah, well . . . the old mod days, y'know . . .'

'Mina again, huh?' said Ava when Kip told her about the interview in Liverpool. 'Anyone'd think you were doing her publicity.'

'Maybe I am.'

'Well, just remember what old Nick Bliss said.'

'OK, Ma. I won't take any candy from the naughty lady.'

On the train to Liverpool, Kip got to know Owen Clark a little better. He'd started the journey with his nose in Nietzsche's *The Birth Of Tragedy*, but the gangling Welshman had interrupted him, questioning the right-on-ness or otherwise of reading the walrus-moustached 'proto-Nazi'. Owen claimed there was a direct and incontrovertible line from Nietzsche through Wagner to Hitler, but Kip disagreed.

Over acrid coffee and Cornish pasties, they talked heatedly of music's role in society.

For Owen, music had a healing, socialising role to play: rock in its heyday had brought people together at festivals and be-ins, had shown them they could live together according to common ideals. For Kip, influenced by John Oldfield and others, music was a dark power which at its best achieved the very opposite of that: it brought people together all right, but as a frenzied and destructive mob. Dionysus always won out over Apollo, intoxication over enlightenment.

'In some ways we're in agreement,' said Kip. 'We both accept that rock and roll involves losing yourself in something bigger than you.'

'But you believe in chaos and I believe in harmony.'

'Well, I just think music unleashes those forces.'

'Like Wagner unleashed in the Nazis.'

'Indeed.'

Owen sat back and gazed for a moment through the window at a hillside strewn with sheep. 'This is where you want to be,' he said. 'Far from your madding bacchic crowds.'

'Miss the old commune, eh?'

'I did live on a commune, actually.'

'Yeah? What happened to it?'

'Too much free love.'

'Ah, Dionysus again.'

'It wasn't the sex. It was that old bourgeois bogeyman jealousy.'

'Maybe people aren't *meant* to live together like that. Wouldn't the history of the human race suggest that?'

'The history of Western Society, perhaps, but what the hell've we got to learn from *that*?'

'So what did you do after the commune fell apart? Move into a semi-detached in Bromley?'

'You wish.'

Kip took a last bite out of his pasty.

Spud was there to meet them at Lime Street, and ushered them towards a taxi. On the way to the hotel, Owen asked Kip to 'fill him in' on Mina. Kip duly gave him a thumbnail sketch. 'She's a goddess, isn't she, Spud?' Spud grunted.

Kip felt nervous as they neared their destination. He hadn't seen Mina since her little fit of pique at Holy Grail Studios. He wondered if the drug rumours were true, and how she'd treat him this time.

The taxi pulled up outside the hotel, Spud jumping out to pay the driver. As Kip and Owen entered the lobby, Rick Stubbs appeared in one of his colonial barfly suits. It was only 1.30, but he already had 5 o'clock shadow on his wet, jowelly face. 'Boy wonder!', he exclaimed in greeting.

'Hi, Rick,' said Kip.

Owen Clark remembered that he'd crossed Rick Stubbs's path before: he'd shot Rick's punk band and sold him the pictures for promotional use.

'Well, if it isn't Owen Clark,' said Rick.

'But it *is* Owen Clark,' said Owen, who had only bad memories of this man.

'Review was killer, Kip,' said Rick, turning away from the photographer.

'My pleasure.'

'Cheque's in the mail, eh?'

Kip forced a smile.

As they turned the corner into 'The Cavern Bar', Kip saw that Dave Mackaye and Boris Salgado were being interviewed by another journalist.

'Where's Mina?' Kip asked.

'In her room, I dare say,' replied Rick. 'What can I get you guys?'

Kip said he'd have a Pils, Owen said nothing.

'I'll give her highness a tinkle, shall I?' said Spud.

'Sounds rather rude, Spud!' tittered Rick. He was clearly on a high, convinced his ship had come in with Mina. Now all the other weeklies were picking up on her, and even some newspapers. Island wanted to do a distribution deal with Tarantula, American A&R men were sniffing around. 'Tell you what,' he said. 'Why don't you talk to Dave and Boris after this chap's finished, and then we'll have some lunch.'

'What about Mina?' asked Kip.

'We'll grab her before the soundcheck.'

'Is there anyone here from Tarantula?'

'Coming down tonight. Why d'you ask?'

'Just wondered.'

'Don't *worry*, Kip, you'll get your interview!'

Dave and Boris made welcoming noises as Kip approached their table. Both men were turned out in rather natty suits, and Boris wore a Homburg.

'Thanks for the review, man,' said Dave, who was smoking a pipe and resembled a young Charles Mingus.

'Dead good, as they say round here,' added Boris.

The interview was a strangely listless affair, as though both Dave and Boris had rehearsed what they were going to say. Boris became vaguely animated when Kip asked him about the production on *La Ronde*, but Dave remained taciturn, puffing on his pipe and offering the occasional 'I 'adn't really thought about it'. All Kip wanted to know about was Mina, but they seemed reluctant to talk about her.

'She's just fine,' said Dave.

'She's resting,' said Boris.

Kip asked them what they'd have been doing if they'd never met Mina.

'Probably working some shitty working men's club,' said Dave.

'It's not so much that,' said Boris. 'More that I'd have missed the opportunity to work with someone who's just so ... unique.' He said the key to *La Ronde* was its collision between Anglo-American sound and European sensibility. 'We have such a wide range of influences. You know, Dave'll be grooving on some idea from *The Black Saint And The Sinner Lady*, I'll find some samba riff coming up from God knows where, and Mina will be singing a line from a song by Joachim Ringelnatz . . .'

'Or the Stones, come to that,' said Dave. 'I mean, it's important to stress that we're not just this kind of ... deranged cabaret band.'

Owen asked when he was going to be able to take his pictures. That was all photographers cared about, thought Kip.

'You'll have to ask Rick or Spud,' said Boris, who'd spotted an A&R man from Island wandering through the lobby. ''Scuse us a second,' he said, and darted out of the bar.

The interview seemed to have reached a natural conclusion when Dave suddenly leaned over and semi-whispered: 'Mina's fine, OK? She's really fine.' It struck Kip as odd, as though Dave felt some compulsion to confess.

'Sure, Dave,' he said.

That Mina was far from 'fine' was immediately apparent when, three hours later, Kip saw her entering the club for the soundcheck. She reminded Kip of the photograph of a famous sixties model leaving a hospital with her wrists bandaged, and seemed almost to be leaning on Rick Stubbs's arm.

Dave and Boris were already onstage, as were Geoff Unwin

and Nigel Hives, the keyboard player and drummer hired for the tour. Kip saw all four of them looking anxiously down at their singer.

Dave put his double bass back in its stand and helped Mina on to the stage. 'Ze lady hess arrived,' muttered Boris into a microphone.

Mina kept her dark glasses on as the band cranked up a peremptory run-through of 'American Friend'. Standing immobile, she sang the lyric in a monotonal drone, devoid of feeling. All the while, Kip watched her with a sense of awe. She seemed to him, messed up or not, more beautiful than ever. Her hair was tied back in a bun, a black scarf draped round her neck.

'There's nothing in this monitor,' she said, pointing to one of the boxes at her feet.

'D'you wanna try a slower number?' shouted a voice from the soundboard.

'Do I hev to?' asked Mina.

'Do a few bars of 'Ghost' or something,' said Boris, who was retuning his semi-acoustic Gibson.

Ten seconds into 'Ghost', Mina stopped the band, saying there was still nothing in one of her monitors. 'How does my guitar sound?' shouted Boris to the engineer.

Kip sat down and scrawled some notes on the back of a napkin: 'A blonde goddess for a dark age . . . tragic diva . . . alone in the spotlight of our desires . . .' Owen sighed that the pictures would now have to wait till the morning.

Finally, the band played the entire way through 'European Nights', which now seemed to incorporate a section from Suicide's 'Diamonds, Fur Coat, Champagne'.' Sounding *very* hot,' said Rick Stubbs, holding a G&T against his bloated stomach.

The local support band, a sort of post-Bunnymen raincoat

outfit, were lugging their gear into the club. A little cacoph-
ony of Scouse wisecracks filled the room.

'Oi, shuddup,' said Spud, who had his feet up on the
soundboard.

'Oooo sorry Mr London rock'n'roll person,' one of them
quipped. 'We didn't know you was a *London* group.'

'Oooo look,' said another. 'They've got a *jerrrnalist* with
them. You gonna be on the cover of the *NME*, then?'

'Why don't you cunts shut it?' said Spud.

'That's all right, Spud,' said Rick, taking over the situation
as it threatened to get out of hand. 'Listen lads, d'you mind
keeping quiet while we finish our soundcheck? Then you can
make as much noise as you like.'

'Don't you "lads" me, you patronising bastard,' said the
lead raincoat.

Kip was finding all this rather hard to believe when Mina,
with a look of intense fury on her face, suddenly descended
from the stage and walked over to the huddle of raincoats.
'Listen, you little shits,' she hissed. 'You fuck around with
me one minute more and I heff you thrown out of the club.
You unnerstand?'

Clearly as impressed as Kip was, the support band promptly
sat down at a table. Kip wrote hurriedly: 'You fuck around
with me one minute more . . .'

The outburst seemed to rejuvenate Mina, who marched
back to the stage in an altogether feistier mood. The
band broke into 'Ugly', with Boris taking a sudden frenzied
solo.

After the soundcheck was over, Mina walked round the
back of the stage and came down towards Kip. He felt his
heart race.

'Hello,' she smiled. 'Did you enjoy our little drama?'

'It was great,' he said.

'All English boy bands are the same,' she said as he sat down. 'Little gangs looking for trouble.'

'Everything all right here?' said Rick Stubbs. 'Get anyone a drink?'

'Brandy,' said Mina.

'I doubt they'll have Courvoisier here, Mina,' said Rick.

'Well, whatever.'

When he'd returned with the drinks, Rick led them upstairs to an office where the raincoat band would be a distant rumble. As they sat down, Kip noticed him laying out a fat line of cocaine on top of a cabinet. Mina ignored this little ceremony, except to say – once the coke was back in her manager's pocket – 'You might have offered Kip some.'

'Oh, not while I'm on duty,' said Kip.

'Well, Rick is supposed to be *on duty* . . .'

'Ah, but coke is an *on duty* drug, isn't it, my dear?' said Rick. 'Unlike certain other substances I could mention.'

Kip watched to see if this produced a rise, but Mina didn't flinch.

'Enjoy your interview,' said Rick as he opened the door.

'Slimeball,' said Mina as it closed behind him.

The interview began stiffly, for Kip was terrified of losing her attention. She talked for some time about *La Ronde*, the choice of cover versions, the writing of the original songs. 'What we tried to do was get away from the romantic lie of love in pop music,' she said. 'In every song on the album, love is just a kind of . . . transaction? Except maybe "Ghost".'

'And you could say it was significant that the only real tenderness comes from someone who's dead.'

'I think only ghosts are capable of this love which everyone babbles about.'

'You believe in ghosts?'

'Of course. Some of my best friends are ghosts.'

'So you've never experienced love or tenderness in your life?'

'Not only me. People think they are in love and it's bullshit. Love in this world is just power and, how you say, owning?'

'Who owns who?'

'Well, nobody owns *me*, I tell you that.'

'But do you own *anybody*?'

'I own *everybody*,' she said, but then smiled.

He asked her about the radical treatment of Roxy Music's 'Bitter-Sweet'.

'Well, we decided to take it all the way. In the original version it's too ... I think you say camp, too sort of Berlin cabaret, especially when he sings the German. So we make it more like Motorhead.'

A little later, when he'd relaxed, Kip took the plunge and asked her about drugs. He said he'd heard 'rumours', and thought they should 'clear this one up for the readers'.

There was a pause as Mina lit a cigarette. 'What drugs?' she asked.

'Um, you tell me.'

'You know, a girl could take this very personally.'

'You don't have to answer, of course. But I have to ask you.'

'The answer is yes, I have taken drugs. The second answer is no, I don't have a drug problem. OK?'

'Fine. Absolutely fine.'

'You watch the show and tell me if a junkie could do what I do. Watch it and tell me that.'

Mina was indeed magnificent that night. From the second she appeared in a top hat, tails and fishnet stockings – her tongue-in-cheek *hommage* to the Dietrich of *Morocco* – she seemed to hold the audience in a vice. Moving effortlessly from the twisted torching of 'Ghost' to the wired funk of 'American Friend', from the cabaret grotesquerie of Brel's 'Tango Funebre' to the hypnotic incantation of 'Evening Of Light', she never relaxed her hold. She was funny, sassy, angry and tortured by turns, and the band soared behind her. Boris slashed out riffs like a Steve Cropper on amyl nitrate, and Dave almost made 'The Death Of Desire' his own. By the time they'd reached the soaring chorus of 'European Nights', Mina had stripped down to a bra and suspenders, her lithe body jerking to the relentless rhythms.

This time there were no catcalls from the crowd, just awe at the power of the sound and the spectacle. Kip stood off to one side in an ecstasy of pride and vindication, scanning the faces in the club and wondering which of them had read his pieces on the band. He stared at Mina as she patrolled the stage, kicking her legs in the air and clasping her breasts in a mock swoon of lust.

Finally, she returned with Boris to sing 'I Thought About You', a racked rendition of a ballad Billie Holiday had recorded shortly before her squalid death:

> But when I pulled down the shade,
> Then I really got blue.
> I peaked through the crack
> And looked at the track
> That wasn't going back to you.
> And what did I do?
> I thought about you . . .

As he listened to the rasping, anguished voice of this girl who said she'd never experienced tenderness, he felt almost sick with desire.

10

Kip was hard at work on his Mina feature when Stevie dropped in to tempt him away from the typewriter. Surrounded by records, books and scrunched-up balls of paper, Kip looked like a consumptive poet in a garret. A musty smell of unwashed clothes hung in the air, and he worked by the dismal light of a 40-watt bulb he'd taken from the loo.

Life in the squat was more bearable now Sancho had moved out. Mick and Carla were still entombed in the end room; Ian Treadwell was doing mime in Covent Garden. In Sancho's place, a strange-looking girl with red corkscrew curls and ginormous breasts had taken up residence. Ruth Frears spent hours boiling up vats of dhal in the kitchen, but at least she didn't come crashing through the front door at six every morning like Sancho.

Stevie, half hoping tasty Ian Treadwell was around, poked his head into Kip's lair. 'Paw!' he exclaimed, clutching his nose. 'Ever heard of a laundrette?' Kip looked up absent-mindedly, finishing the sentence he was typing. Consumed by the piece, he'd scarcely seen anyone since returning from Liverpool the week before. It was as though he'd been entrusted with the task of spreading the word of some new prophet. Pictures of Mina bedecked the walls of his room, and *La Ronde* played incessantly on his secondhand Trio sound system.

'For fuck's sake, Kip,' said Stevie. 'When you gonna give it a rest?'

'You ever heard of deadlines, Stephen?'

'How many drafts have you already written of this soddin' story?'

'Three.'

'All those words on account of some Teutonic tart with a smack problem.'

'How do *you* know she's got a smack problem? Christ, you're as bad as fucking John Blake or something.'

'*You* were the one told me, yer daft git.'

Kip hammered out another sentence.

'I mean,' said Stevie, 'you're treatin' her like she was the second coming or sommat.'

'Well, maybe she is.'

'No, Kip, she's not. She may be many things, but she is not the second coming of anything.'

'We'll see.'

Plonking himself down on the bed, Stevie continued to mull over Kip's apparent obsession with the girl they'd seen in Camden just a few months before. Of course, it was conceivable that the obsession was simply about Kip's ambition, his desire to make a name for himself as a writer. Or perhaps he derived some vicarious thrill from his championing of the singer: because he'd 'discovered' her, he imagined in some deluded way that he'd *created* her. Doubtless there was some truth in both these theories, though neither of them quite explained the pictures on the wall. Kip's room, Stevie decided, was really no different from the bedrooms of thousands of Adam Ant or Haircut 100 fans.

'Would you like to fuck her?' he asked finally.

'Would I what?'

'You 'eard me.'

'Of course I would,' said Kip, looking round at his friend.

'Has she got a boyfriend?'

'I don't really know. She doesn't seem the lovey-dovey type.'

'You can say that again. And if she *is* a junkie . . .'

'*If* . . .'

'. . . then she probably wouldn't be too interested anyway.'

'Maybe not.'

'Maybe she's gay.'

'Could be.'

'Does that turn you on?'

'Um . . .'

'Howz about S&M? Mina in full dominatrix clobber, standing over you with a whip . . .'

'Sounds delightful.'

'I hope you'll say that in yer piece.'

Kip wondered whether Dez Frippett would make the piece a cover story. He tried to imagine Owen's pictures, snapped beside the Mersey on the morning after the show: the blonde icon flanked by her dark sidemen.

'What's yer next assignment?' asked Stevie.

'My what?'

'What you doing after you've finished the piece?'

'D'you know, I hadn't really thought about it.'

Kip took his piece into *Cover* that Thursday. He immediately spotted Ava, who was in conference with Joe Grout. Pamela Motown noticed him and asked if he fancied reviewing 'the sad old Rolling Stones' at Wembley.

The office was once again filling up for the editorial

meeting. Baggy-trousered Malcolm Reeves was awaiting the arrival of Dave Duncan, back from his third trip to New York that year. Don Barstow was putting the finishing touches to a piece about 23 Skidoo, and Jah Moody was humming an old Horace Andy tune. At five minutes to three, Nick Bliss walked in, begrimed with cigarette ash. With him was a reddish-headed, unassuming-looking character in a duffle coat. It was John Oldfield.

'I thought he never came into the office,' Kip whispered loudly in Ava's ear.

'*Almost* never,' said Ava.

Kip continued talking but he had eyes only for Oldfield, who appeared to be asking Jah Moody something about the legendary Studio One label. Ava sensed the awe with which Kip was staring across the room and left him to it.

To the amazement not just of Kip but of almost everyone else in the office, Oldfield proceeded to follow Ava into the meeting. The only person not visibly amazed was Dave Duncan, who was more concerned with ensuring that everyone knew about his New York trip by hurling duty free cigarette cartons across the room.

'Yer fags, Malcy!' he shouted.

Dez asked if he'd had a good trip.

'Bit of a drag, actually,' said the Scotsman.

'Poor Dave,' Ava sighed. 'Life must be so hard for you.'

Clearing his throat, Dez launched into his standard periodic rant about late copy, inflated expense forms, people not pulling their weight. He welcomed John Oldfield to the meeting, saying it was a rare pleasure to see him. The new issue, however, was not a rare pleasure. 'Hardly surprising circulation's going down if we're producing shit like this.'

There were two or three muted howls, both of protest and of agreement. Nick Bliss wanted to know what 'fucking

Imagination' were doing on the cover, which prompted an immediate charge of racism from Malcolm Reeves. Don Barstow was indignant that his Blue Orchids piece had been 'slashed to pieces'. Even Jah Moody looked perturbed, saying he couldn't find his 'Dub Waves' column anywhere in the paper. 'Oh yeah, sorry about that,' said Joe Grout in a thoroughly unremorseful voice.

After five more minutes of fruitless reproaches, Dez turned his attention to the future. Dave Duncan was doing a big piece on salsa; Nick Bliss was due to interview Mick Jagger, no less. Other names being floated about were Prince, the Clash, Tom Verlaine and the Au Pairs. 'I'd like to do something on this woman Diamanda Galas,' said Don Barstow. 'She makes Mina look like Melanie.' Kip bristled.

It was John Oldfield who spoke next. He seemed paralytically shy, but managed to mumble something about 'desire in pop'. 'I've got this idea,' he said, 'for a long piece about . . . well, about sex, I suppose.' Kip couldn't help noticing that the duffle-coated recluse then blushed to the roots of his red hair. Dez quickly came to the rescue. 'Sounds terrific, John,' he said. 'Shall we speak afterwards?' Oldfield nodded and immediately began ferreting around in an old Safeway bag. Out fell a book called *Language, Sexuality, and Subversion*.

There was a silence, after which Ava asked who was going to be on the next cover.

'We're going with Mina,' said Dez. 'Owen's pix are great, and Kip's piece . . . well, we'll have to see, won't we?'

It was Kip's turn to blush, though not quite to the roots.

11

Kip's odd sort of affair with Ava Cadaver was on its last legs when he agreed to accompany her to Manchester for the opening of a new club.

During the coach journey up the M1, Ava kept pressing up against him and nuzzling his ear. Since he had his nose stuck in Roland Barthes's *A Lover's Discourse*, he found the discrepancy between her attentions and the playfully cerebral prose almost too much to bear. And when he read that 'the lover's anxiety' is 'the fear of a mourning which has already occurred, at the very origin of love, from the moment when I was first "ravished"', he thought only of Mina.

Ava said 'Jesus' and slumped back into her seat.

Old couples munched sandwiches in lay-bys, cows chomped grass in the shadows of power plants. Kip calculated that Mina must be in Rotterdam by now. Had she seen his cover story, 'Siren of Desire', he wondered? He imagined her reading it, her thoughts of him as she took in each sentence.

'I have projected myself into the other with such power,' he read in Barthes, 'that when I am without the other I cannot recover myself, regain myself . . .'

The opening of the club seemed a subdued affair, especially when a painfully shy girl band flown in from the South Bronx took the stage. As they played, a chirpy Mancunian voice asked if he was Kip Wilson. He said he was.

'I bought the Mina album and it were shite,' said the boy.

'You think so?' said Kip with feigned politeness. It was Ava who dragged him away, already well attuned to that one-too-many tone in the English male voice. 'Looks like your Mina campaign's really taking off,' she couldn't resist saying.

As it happened, Ava's jealousy had rather abated in recent weeks; she herself had developed a crush on the lead singer of a Goth band called Crucifiction. (The boy had even called her a couple of times, though she couldn't help wondering if that was merely because of her usefulness to his band.) But her pride was still smarting somewhat from Kip's fixation with Mina, and she wanted him to know that.

Arriving back in London as the sun was coming up over the city, she thought she'd give Kip one more chance to demonstrate some affection. The dawn light hurt his eyes and he wished Ava wasn't there.

Stevie had once asked if it was true that all American girls gave great head, and Kip had said it was. But when they were under his rather grubby duvet, he tried to imagine that it was Mina going down on him.

The morning light was coming through the green sheet that was Kip's curtain.

The relationship petered out. Kip and Ava talked when he came into *Cover*, but he was increasingly distant. Even Dez noticed the change in him. 'Whassup, man?' he'd say. 'Yer fire's gone out.' Ironically, Dez put it all down to the 'break-up' with Ava. 'Pity about that,' he'd say with an avuncular sigh. 'Nice girl, even if she does look like Morticia Addams.'

Stevie, too, wondered if Kip hadn't crossed some invisible line in his Mina obsession. A strange look came into the boy's eye whenever he mentioned her – and he mentioned her with alarming regularity. 'I think Mina would like that,' he'd say, or: 'It would be interesting to hear Mina cover that song.' He'd spot a girl in Vinyl Dementia and whisper behind a cupped hand: 'That girl has exactly the same build as Mina.'

It all came to a head when the two friends went to see the Stones at Wembley. At first, Kip had seemed genuinely amused by the idea of reviewing the show. He'd thought back to the epiphany of Earl's Court six years before, wanting to make his own statement about the travesty that was Mick Jagger in the post-punk era. But when the greying veterans emerged in the early evening light, he could scarcely be bothered to take his usual notes. After seven songs he actually sat down on the ground.

'Whatcha doing down there?' bellowed Stevie after a particularly painful rendition of 'Let's Spend The Night Together'. 'Thought you were supposed to be reviewing this.'

'It's too boring,' Kip replied listlessly.

'What the fuck did you expect?'

Stevie wanted to say more, but he was drowned out by Bill Wyman and Charlie Watts kick-starting the next number. By the end of the set, Kip was curled up in a foetal ball. Stevie wondered if he was coming down from speed or withdrawing from something altogether stronger. He'd had a brief scene with a junkie – 'my Joe D'Allesandro', he'd called him – and remembered vividly the innocent sleep that preceded full-blown withdrawal.

But Kip had simply switched off. Somehow he would produce the requisite seven hundred words for Pamela Motown the next morning, and then go back to figuring out ways to see Mina again.

'You wanna eat?' asked Stevie as they fell out of the Black-Hole-of-Calcutta tube.

'Sure,' said Kip.

Washing down his curry with lager, Kip slowly emerged from his depression. After three quarters of an hour he'd managed to down three pints to Stevie's one and was slamming his fists on the table while singing Rolling Stones songs. Had the restaurant not been empty, Stevie might have led him gently out into the street. But the waiters were used to worse on Friday nights.

Several toasts to the Stones later, Kip was lurching his way back to Paddington. There was no one at home besides Ruth Frears, whom Kip discovered sitting in the kitchen with a novel and a mug of camomile tea. Ruth had never seen Kip drunk before and felt slightly alarmed. After watching him stumble about trying to make a coffee, she offered to help him.

'Why, that would be *most* kind,' he burped. He liked watching her pad about the kitchen in bare feet; her breasts made him think of Russ Meyer movies. She poured boiling water into a cracked Roland Rat mug.

'How were the Stones?' she asked, bringing the coffee to the table.

'Unspeakable,' said Kip.

'Are you reviewing it for your paper?'

'Don't remind me, for fuck's sake!'

'They are getting on a bit, aren't they.'

'They're the walking bloody dead is what they are. Some-one should put them out of their misery.'

'Is that what you're going to say?'

'What else *can* you say?'

Kip felt sick and threw back the coffee in an effort to sober up. 'Oh Ruth,' he groaned. 'I'm so fucking lonely.'

Ruth assumed that her squatmate was referring to the break-up with Ava. 'Oh dear,' she said. 'Must be very difficult seeing her in the office all the time.'

Ruth cleared her throat as Kip buried his head in his hands. 'Are you seeing anyone else?' she asked.

'Actually, I was saving myself for you.'

'Oh sure.'

'Scout's honour.'

'Ki-ip,' said Ruth, unsure how to take this.

'Only you can save me,' said Kip as he slumped to the floor. The next thing Ruth heard was the first verse of 'Help Me Make It Through The Night', delivered in a tuneless croak. She gave an uneasy laugh. 'You've got to help me, Ruth,' said Kip.

'Kip, you should go to bed.'

'I'll go to *your* bed . . .'

'That's not what I meant.'

'I want to see those fantastic breasts of yours.'

'Well, they're not for viewing.'

'Oh go on,' he said, rolling around on the floor.

'So much for your broken heart!' She carried the mugs over to the sink.

'How can you *say* that?'

'Kip, I'm going to bed. I'll see you tomorrow.'

'Leave me to die here, alone and forgotten.'

'Don't worry, I'll call the undertaker in the morning.'

'You'll never get over the guilt!'

'I'll manage.'

Kip's Stones review, a free-ranging blend of fantasy and vitriol, had already come in for copious criticism when Dez Frippett summoned him the following Thursday.

'Kip,' said Dez, 'I have to tell you that if I'd seen your

Stones review before the paper went to bed on Monday I'd
have yanked it straight away. I mean, did you actually *go* to
Wembley?'

'Of course I did.'

'Well, I'd be surprised if our readers believed that, honestly.
You barely mention a single song they played, and there's no
mention at all of the J. Geils Band, who I understand were
one of the support bands. *Bloodshot* was a classic album, you
know.'

'Sorry, Dez.'

'I want to know what's going on with you. I know you've
split up with Ava, I know it's been a difficult few weeks, but
I can't sort of mollycoddle you forever.'

'I know, Dez. For some reason I just went off the deep
end with this one.'

'See, John Oldfield name-dropping Ronald Barts is one
thing, but this is just bloody out-to-lunch.'

Kip said nothing.

'I'm gonna give you one more chance,' Dez said as he
placed his cowboy-booted feet on the desk. 'I've just had a
communication from my old mate Rick Stubbs, though
between you and me the guy was always a pain in the
sphincter. Rick says that Mina has formed a new band and is
gonna tour the States with them. Apparently the album is
already very big on the college circuit over there.'

'Formed a new band?' Kip was incredulous.

'Broken away from those guys, hired two guitar players,
the works.'

'I can't believe it.'

'Anyway, and this has got to remain our little secret, she's
agreed to give us an interview, but it's got to be with you.
She won't talk to anyone else.'

Kip felt his heart pounding.

'Normally I couldn't possibly countenance that sort of request. You take whoever we assign to interview you or you piss off. In this case, though, we really need her in the paper.'

'You mean, go to America?'

'I mean go to America, which means you have to write me a piece I can understand and our readers can understand, and then I won't regret making this decision.'

'No problem, Dez.'

'Attaboy, Kip.'

12

Kip took the train from Paddington to Exeter, carrying the morning suit he'd hired for Gemma's wedding.

Sheila Wilson was at Exeter St David's to meet him in her battered Austin Allegro. A strange mixture of girlish excitement and menopausal fatigue played across her face as she told Kip about the arrangements for the wedding. 'You will be nice to Gemma on her special day, won't you?' she asked.

''Course I will, Mum,' he said.

'So darling, how *is* it all going? Are you still living in bohemian splendour?'

'I'm still in the squat, Mum.'

'Yes, but it sounds so depressing, doesn't it. Squatting.'

'Oh, it's all right. But you'll be pleased to know Sancho's moved out.'

'Well, I'm sure that's for the best. And how about all your writing? *Terribly* exciting.'

'Well, I'm going to America in a couple of weeks,' he said as matter-of-factly as possible.

'To *America*! Darling, that *is* exciting.'

'Yes, I'm going on tour with that singer I told you about.'

'Now yes, remind me. Was she the one that sang Kurt Weill songs?'

'One Kurt Weill song, yes. Anyway, seems like I picked a winner there, because her album's doing really well in the States.'

'Well, how absolutely thrilling, darling.'

Soon they were pulling into the little gravelled driveway that led to the crumbling vicarage where Kip had grown up. Michael Wilson looked mildly irritated as he wandered back to the house from the marquee on the lawn.

'The return of the prodigal rocker,' he muttered as the Allegro pulled up beside him.

'Hello, Dad,' Kip managed.

'Darling, they're sending Kip to *America*. Can you believe it?'

'Can I believe it? Is it a trick question?'

'Michael, do at least pretend to sound excited.'

'Overrated place, America. Used to lecture there, y'know. Ghastly little cities in the midwest.'

'Yes, Dad.'

'Still, with any luck you'll manage to avoid Toledo, Ohio, so you should be OK.'

'Yes, Dad.'

'Kip, you must be starving,' said Sheila. 'Come in and say hello to Gemma, and then we'll have some supper.'

Kip dutifully knocked on his sister's door, only to find her fretting over a tiny tear in her wedding dress. She presented a cold cheek for a kiss, then yelled down the hall at her mother.

Every time Kip thought about America he got butterflies. Dez's words echoed through his mind: 'She wants to do another interview, but she won't talk to anyone on the paper except you.' And now Dave and Boris were gone, there was just Mina – and her new band, whoever they were.

It was just the Wilsons' luck that Gemma's wedding day should turn out to be overcast. At least Michael Wilson felt slightly less resentful about the money he'd shelled out for the marquee. Kip crawled out of bed and shaved to the sound of *La Ronde*.

At breakfast, Kip's uncle Andrew managed to spill his coffee all over the table, provoking an impatient outburst from his brother, who sat as usual at the head of the table. Kip noticed that his father was now reading the *Spectator* rather than the *New Statesman*.

Gemma appeared, looking rather haggard as she descended the stairs with her mother. Andrew Wilson, rising uneasily to his feet, pronounced that his niece looked 'quite ravishing'.

'Wonder what Jeremy's stag night was like,' said Michael with an impish grin.

'They'd better not have done anything too wild,' said Gemma.

'No risk of that, surely,' her father couldn't resist.

'Oh, Dad, he's not a *complete* wimp.'

'Now if you want a *stag* night,' said Michael, 'you should have seen what your old man got up to.'

'I'd rather not have to think about it, thanks.'

'Well, it was glorious, wasn't it, Andrew?'

Actually, Andrew Wilson visibly squirmed at the memory of it, since he'd wound up being pinned down by Michael's drunken cronies while an elderly Welsh prostitute lowered herself on to his face.

'Oh well,' smirked Michael, 'perhaps the breakfast table's not really the place to rekindle those happy memories.' Andrew breathed a sigh of relief.

The rest of the morning was spent in various states of hysteria by all concerned. Kip himself stood in front of a mirror trying to convince himself he didn't look preposterous in his morning suit. Christ, if Mina could see him now – could see this whole middle-class farce – would she ever talk to him again?

He found it hard to stay awake during the service at St Crispin's-on-the-Weald. Only a certain sadistic pleasure in watching his sister commit herself body and soul to the feckless Jeremy Bagshaw kept his eyes open through the solemn nonsense wafting from the mouth of the Rev. Alan Lunt. Various awful cousins and in-laws had crowded out the little church: overweight matrons in pink bonnets, balding colleagues of his father's in inky blue suits.

When it was all over, everyone made their way back to the vicarage for lunch. To Kip's slight horror, among the various guests milling around the garden was none other than Tim 'Scummy' Mackinnon, looking annoyingly dapper in an obviously tailored suit.

'Well well,' Scummy said on beholding his fellow 'Old Dunster'. He turned to a leggy blonde in a red mini skirt and said: 'Honey bunch, I want you to meet the bride's bro, the guy who drove us all mad playing punk records at school.' The girl glanced vacantly in Kip's direction as Scummy went on: 'Yes, this is the great Kip Wilson, world authority on rock trivia, a legend in his own . . .'

'And to what do we owe *your* appearance at this happy event?' Kip interjected.

'Don't ask me, I'm just tagging along with Andrea.'

'Well, how does Andrea come to be here?'

'Don't even know that, I'm afraid.'

'I suppose I should ask you what you're up to, since you're obviously doing all right for yourself.'

'Doing fairly nicely, as it goes – antiques. You?'

'I'm, um, a music journalist.'

'But of course you are! What else would you be!'

Kip scowled, then asked what had happened to Bruce Frith.

'Went abroad, I believe. Working in New York or something.'

'You didn't keep up with him?'

'Nope.'

'And Andrea's your girlfriend?'

'Wife, if you please.'

'Gosh.'

'Quite.'

'Well, Scummy, I won't say it's a pleasure seeing you again, because it isn't. But take care anyway.'

'Indeed, Kip, and the best of luck in your career as a . . . what do they call it, rock critic?'

'That's right, Scummy. And the best of luck in the bric-à-brac business.'

It wasn't long before the old relic who was serving as Master of Ceremonies could be heard calling people in to the marquee for the cake-cutting and speechifying part of the ordeal. Kip was soon wincing as Michael Wilson adjusted his pince-nez and began talking in drearily derogatory tones about Gemma and Jeremy. Being fairly drunk, he managed to refer to his new son-in-law as 'Gemmary' at least twice before forcing himself to wish the happy couple 'the very best of whatever it is that marriage is supposed to bring'. Jeremy then uttered a few grovelling words of his own, followed by his even wetter best man, a chinless stockbroker by the name of Simon Bole. 'I won't go into what we did last night,' Bole said with a knowing snigger.

Back in his room, Kip lay on his bed and drank from a half-empty bottle of champagne. As the guests began once again to twitter away in the garden, their voices were drowned out by the sound of Mina intoning the first verse of 'The Love Market'.

13

On the flight to New York, Kip drank a Bloody Mary and felt a kind of wild elation.

He'd managed to gather a little more information about Mina's new band, who were called the Sacred Monsters of Desire and were made up of various ex-'No Wave' musicians from New York. He'd even obtained a demo tape of new material, which sounded something like Glenn Branca crossed with Big Brother & the Holding Company.

Which was partly how Kip came to be reading a biography of Janis Joplin – or would have been had Owen Clark not fallen asleep on it. The excessively tall photographer had nearly missed the flight out of Gatwick, and was now recovering from the frantic last stages of his train journey.

The in-flight movie was some cheesy family adventure featuring the most obnoxiously cute children Kip had ever seen. As if to counteract their golden hair and gleaming smiles, he listened once again to the tape of Mina's new songs. Appropriately enough, the first track had a working title of 'Art Of Darkness', which was a cheap play on words but one fully justified by its violent, imploding music. Kip even thought he could make out a reference to Aleister Crowley in the lyric.

The three remaining songs were less brutal: one of them, 'Consumed', struck Kip as the loveliest thing he'd ever heard Mina sing. 'If we can't get that one on the radio,' Rick had said, 'I'll personally nobble the promo guys.' As for the Sacred Monsters, while they perhaps lacked the subtlety of Mackaye and Salgado – Rick had proved evasive on the subject of the pair's departure – they made up for that with the power of their playing.

Owen Clark looked refreshed when he finally stirred.

'Could I get my book back now?' Kip smiled, pulling *Buried Alive* from under Owen's arm.

'God, sorry,' said Owen, noting the book's title. 'Janis Joplin?'

'Yeah. I'm sort of interested in her.'

'Saw her once, but I was tripping. What's the book like?'

'Pretty sad story. She was fucked up *without* the drugs.'

'Some connection with Mina?'

'Maybe.'

'Just so long as she doesn't bugger us about like she did in Liverpool.'

The Westchester Hotel, a stone's throw from Times Square, was not the swankiest joint in town. But Kip was happy just to feel the blanket of humidity on his skin, the shriek of police sirens in his ears.

'I suppose we should buzz that awful manager of hers,' said Owen in the lobby.

'Or Spud,' suggested Kip.

'Is Mr Stubbs in, d'you know?' Owen asked when they'd got the attention of the crusty old desk clerk.

'He just left the hotel, sir. Are you checkin' in?'

'Might as well. The names are Clark and Wilson.'

A minute went by as the man tried to find their names.

'Always the same,' sighed Owen. 'Travel three thousand miles and some git like Rick Stubbs has forgotten to book you in.'

Kip cleared his throat. 'Perhaps we could try Mina's room,' he said.

'Could do. Can you try Mina, please?'

'Mina who?'

'The singer Mr Stubbs looks after.'

'I'm not sure I should disturb her, sir.'

'Well look, we've come all the way from England to interview her. I'm sure she wouldn't want us hanging around here.'

'One moment,' said the clerk.

As the phone rang, Kip had visions of Mina naked, Mina overdosed, Mina fucking her bass player. Then the clerk was saying 'Oh miss, very sorry to disturb you . . .'

Kip's heart thudded.

'They say they should have been booked into the hotel by Mr Stubbs, but Mr Stubbs just left the hotel.'

A pause.

'You want me to send 'em up? Sure thing, miss.'

'We're in,' said Owen, picking up his bags and cameras.

'Take the elevator to the seventh floor and room 703 is immediately to your left.'

A minute later they were knocking on Mina's door. There was no sound within, not even the everpresent white noise of American television. Kip knocked again, his heart in his throat.

Finally the door opened, and Mina emerged from the darkness. The dishevelled blonde hair all but concealed her face, but her eyes blinked in the faint light of the corridor as she beckoned them in.

'Sorry, we didn't mean to wake you,' said Kip.

'You didn't,' she said, pushing her hands back through her hair. 'Please sit down, guys.'

Kip drank in everything he saw: stockings slung across the back of a chair, a half-empty bottle of brandy on the TV set, magazines spread across the floor.

'Wait till I see that stupid fuck Rick,' Mina said as she searched for some cigarettes. 'You wanna drink?'

'Why not?' said Owen.

As Mina poured brandy into a pair of coffee cups, her robe almost fell open.

'How's it all going with the new band?' Kip asked.

'Good,' was all she'd say.

'What happened with Dave and Boris, if you don't mind my asking?'

'Is this the interview already?' she smiled. 'I tell you everything in good time. The story of Mina and Dave and Boris and the Sacred Monsters of Desire.'

'I love the new stuff.'

'Yes it's good, but not finished.'

'"Consumed" is amazing.'

'Thank you.'

'Have you been to New York before?' asked Owen, who was standing at the window.

'No, I have never been.'

'You like it?'

'It's OK. Better than London.'

The phone rang: Rick had returned to rectify what he called his 'little oversight'. Except that there was only one room left in the hotel, so they'd have to share for the night. Rick asked Mina if she still wanted to see the 'avant-metal' band in which her new guitarist and collaborator was moon-lighting that night. Cupping a hand over the mouthpiece,

she relayed the information to Kip and Owen. Kip nodded
that he'd like to go.

'They wanna go,' said Mina. 'I get changed, we meet in
twenty minutes.' Kip and Owen took this as their cue to
check into their own room.

Rick was leaning on the desk as they stepped out of the
lift. 'Guys, how'll you ever forgive me?' he said.

'We won't,' said Owen.

'Needless to say it was Spud's fault.'

'Passing the buck again.'

'Naturally! Tell you what, we'll eat on the way, dinner on
me.'

'Very sporting of you.'

'Owen Clark, the man who never forgets and never
forgives. How's old Dez, by the by?'

'He's fine.'

'So glad we managed to fix up this trip. You're not going
to *believe* the new show. I mean, this band is *red* hot.'

'OK, gennelmen,' said the old clerk. 'You're in room
three-twelve. Please make sure to leave your keys at the
desk.'

Rick's little party threaded their way through the dense mass
of scenesters who'd come to see Ugly Blood. People stared
hard as Mina walked past, and Kip stared back at them. He
was thrilled just to be seen with her, the girl whose beauty
and notoriety had already propelled her into the *Village Voice*
and the *New York Rocker*.

When they'd sat down, a dark, unshaven man attached
himself to their table. He turned out to be Richard Diltz, a
rock writer with a major bee in his bonnet about what he
called 'plastic limey pop'.

'*Cover*, huh?' he began as Howlin' Wolf's 'How Many

More Years' came over the sound system. 'That the rag which puts, like, Haircut 100 on the cover every other week?'

'No, it isn't,' said Kip.

'Maybe I'm gettin' confused with some bitchin' band like The Human League. I'll never understand how you limeys keep falling for that same plastic shit. Ever since you foisted the fuckin' Beatles on the world you've produced these sappy, wimpy little bands . . .'

'So what decent bands has New York produced recently?'

'*This* band, for a start.'

'Yeah?'

'Yeah, and I notice the young lady at your table's had to come here to find some decent musicians.' He leaned over towards Mina. 'Hey, *fraulein*! Your limey journo pal and me are debatin' as to exactly what you're doin' here in my beloved hometown.'

Mina inspected Diltz's face. 'Well, not talking to pricks like you, for one thing,' she said. Kip grinned.

'Oh right. So maybe you're en route to South America or somewhere to hook up with some of your Nazi pals.'

Owen was ready to rise from his seat, but Mina was already on her feet. The next thing Kip knew, she was emptying a beer over Richard Diltz's head. Several people around the table applauded wildly, and Kip joined in. Only Rick Stubbs, concerned about 'media repercussions', refrained from clapping along. As the humiliated Diltz shuffled off, moreover, Rick followed him to the bathroom.

'See what a good manager he is,' said Mina.

'Pity I didn't have my camera,' said Owen.

Ugly Blood were just making their way on to the cramped stage. To Kip's surprise, they looked like a bunch of Ivy League preppies, not the scuzzy Lower East Side junkies he'd expected.

They broke into their opening number with a formidable crash, sounding like Throbbing Gristle crossed with primal Black Sabbath. The bassist screamed into a mic as the two guitarists produced vicious squalls of feedback, and the drummer took random solos on a kit which looked as if it had just been rescued from the pawnshop.

Slowly, Kip's jet lag kicked in. He began to drown in the relentless lava flow of black noise, longing to sink into sleep. 'I think we rather overestimated Kip's tolerance for this stuff,' said Rick between numbers.

'Tell him that was nothing,' said Mina. 'The Sacred Monsters will . . . *obliterate* him.'

THE SACRED MONSTERS
OF DESIRE
Ritz, New York

The hallmark of genius is its restlessness: never staying in one place for longer than it takes to trash it. Scarcely had we gotten (as they say here) used to the band which made *La Ronde* when, lo and behold! Mina flees to America and takes off on a totally new tangent.

And what she has done, this most untame-able of pop goddesses, is put together a 100% bona fide ROCK AND ROLL band, with two guitars, bad attitudes and the odd mop of shoulder-length hair.

With the unexpected success of *La Ronde* over here, Mina's show at the Ritz The-a-ter brings people flocking out of the downtown shadow-world to see what all the fuss is about. Here they all come, drugged and dressed in black, itching to see the new High Priestess, curious to know who or what her Sacred Monsters are. I'm no less curious myself.

What the Sacred Monsters are is: Lee Krantz on guitar, Jimmi Colena on guitar, Bo Hartman on drums and Dupont Greer on bass. There are no keyboards or backing tracks here, just a bunch of Marshall amps and a whole lot of sonic terrorism. Metal? Not quite, because there's too much else going on in the sound of this band to give it that metallic k.o. punch. On t'other hand, there's a mildly tongue-in-cheek cover of Sabbath's 'War Pigs' about halfway through the set, so maybe we'll see Mina duetting with Lemmy yet.

After a short support set by some jingle-jangle brigade out of Noo Joizey, Dupont Greer takes the stage and starts hammering away at a beat-up Fender Precision bass. Nothing else happens for a while. Then Mina *crawls* on to the stage on all fours, her face partially obscured by the most enormous sunglasses you've ever seen. Greer's bass figures, feedbacking wildly in his amp, build to a growling inferno, and gradually his fellow Monsters wander on. Mina is still on the floor, pinned down by a single ice-blue spotlight.

I'd seen Lee Krantz the night before, moonlighting with noise guerrillas Ugly Blood, but nothing could have prepared me for the blitzkrieg of sound he and Jimmi Colena manage to generate on the opening 'Art Of Darkness', a song which immediately marks the birth of the New Mina. Rising up from the floor, the lady herself grabs her mic stand and starts swaying to the waves of electric power surging behind her. Bo Hartman, dreadlocked crazyman in a gold baseball cap, pounds out the most ear-shattering beat, and it's all one can do not to give oneself up to a bout of shameless headbanging.

Mina's voice has undergone a transformation of sorts, too. There's a touch of Joplin's anguished howl in her pipes now, like a desert wind blowing through a heap of bones. When the band feeds through in to 'Ugly' or the new 'Consumed', she raises the hairs on the back of your neck with what I can only describe as a chilling death rattle in her throat. 'Consumed', due for release on a forthcoming EP, will be one of the Songs Of The Year. As a testament to obsession – desire as fatal disease – it trumps anything on *La Ronde*, laying to rest any fears that Mina would not be able to deliver without her former accomplices.

The set moves through the old and the new, through a remade 'Bitter-Sweet' and a remodelled 'Poison Doll'. Introducing 'European Nights', Mina says: 'This is for my old life.' Neatly if predictably, she follows it up with 'American Friend' – but not like you've ever heard it before. There's precious little *funk* in it now, which perhaps tells us something about her view of America now she's finally here. The GI Joe of the song has become Everyman-as-neighbourhood-psycho: there's one on every block, back from 'Nam, nerves shredded.

The Sacred Monsters wind up in a welter of feedback and criss-cross rhythms, driving us towards sonic meltdown. Possessed by the sheer power she's conjured from the bowels of rock, Mina hurls herself around the stage, eyes closed in a trance. It is impossible to take your eyes off her.

Sacred and monstrous indeed.

Kip Wilson

14

The triumph of the Ritz behind them, the Sacred Monsters were heading into the American unknown. The heartland opened before them, an endless trail of motels and franchises stretching across Pennsylvania, Ohio, Indiana.

On the bus, the thought came to Kip that his Mina feature might be nothing short of a love letter, that she would only have to read between its lines to know the intensity of his feelings for her. Had she not, in any case, already sensed those feelings? Why else request that he alone interview her?

There was only one thing troubling Kip, and that was the apparent *frisson* between Mina and Jimmi Colena. A strapping, olive-complexioned boy from Brooklyn, Jimmi was Kip's idea of a woman's idea of sexy. Furthermore, the guy exhibited all the standard traits of the Italian 'ladies' man', hovering around Mina like a bee around a flower. Surely it would only be a matter of time before she succumbed to him. 'How much we need the other's desire,' Kip had read in *A Lover's Discourse*, 'even if this desire is not addressed to us.'

The plan was to stay with the tour till Chicago, where Mina's 3,500-capacity show had sold out within hours. It gave Kip three days and as many gigs to interview her and each of the Sacred Monsters.

Bo Hartman, the dreadlocked Canadian drummer, struck him as the most approachable of the bunch, so he began with him after breakfast at the Pittsburgh Days Inn, moving on to Lee Krantz and Dupont Greer on the bus. Krantz was the least forthcoming Monster, cagey about the group's formation and prickly about the music scene in New York. His button-down shirts seemed at once a defiance of rock's standard dress code and a genuine expression of his Ivy League origins. The Dallas-born Greer, who claimed to have played with Cherry Vanilla, was a dyed-in-the-wool bread-head with little to say about Mina or any other subject. 'Ah jist play the bass, don't ask no questions, don't tell no lies,' he rasped as he lit his twentieth Kool of the day.

Kip intentionally saved Jimmi Colena till last. In an uninviting diner five miles over the Illinois state line, he turned on his tape recorder and ran through the basics: what bands Jimmi had played with, how he'd hooked up with Mina in the first place. 'What exactly were your impressions of Mina when you met her?' he asked.

'My first impressions?!' said the guitarist. 'I thought she was a babe!' It was as Kip had feared. 'I mean, she ain't the sorta broad you see around Brooklyn, that's for sure. It's like she was real classy but real . . . bizarre?'

'What about the music?'

'Well, I never played anything like this before. First time I heard the album I dint think I *could* play it. But I listened and now I think it's pretty cool.'

Kip by this point had decided Jimmi was a complete meathead. 'How're you finding the shows?' he asked.

'Wild, man. Don't tell her this, but I get so turned on durin' the set, sometimes I have to thank the Lord for makin' me a guitar player. If you get my meaning.'

'Whereas if you were a flautist . . .'

'If I was a *what*?'

'It doesn't matter.'

Over Jimmi's shoulder, Kip could see Mina herself, her eyes masked by sunglasses.

'Thanks for your time, Jimmi,' he said. 'Hope the rest of the tour goes well.'

'You got it, man. Be sure and give my love to London!'

By the time the bus was rolling into the Windy City, Mina had become a seriously hip name to bandy about in 'alternative rock' circles. They arrived at the Marriott Hotel to find a small posse of aspiring decadents gathered in the lobby to welcome her. *La Ronde*, it seemed, was breaking into *Billboard*'s Top Hundred Albums chart.

One result of all this was that Kip's interview with Mina was put on hold to allow Rick to deal with the American press. It meant that Kip would have to continue on with the tour, possibly all the way to LA. Owen was furious, insisting Rick arrange a photo session that afternoon.

Kip was heading for his room in the Marriott when suddenly Mina herself stepped out of a lift. He felt himself blush as he tried to appear calm. She asked if he wanted to come to her room for a drink.

Ten minutes later, a can of Michelob in his hand, he was waiting for her to come out of the bathroom.

Rick Stubbs called and asked where she was. 'And what are *you* doing in her room?' he added. Spud called to give her the soundcheck time.

Another five minutes went by before Mina, her mood clearly altered by some chemical, reappeared. She asked who'd called.

'Spud called to say the soundcheck's at five, and Rick probably just called to hassle you.'

She gave a slight groan and flopped on to the bed.

'You OK?' ventured Kip.

'No.'

He wasn't sure what to say.

'Now I suppose you will put this in your piece, that you saw me shoot up drugs or something.'

'I'd never do anything to hurt you,' he said, and realised how sappy it sounded. She said he was sweet.

He stared at her supine form, the eyes closed but the mouth ever so slightly open. He remembered her using the word *sehnsucht* to convey a particular kind of longing, and thought he must be feeling it now.

But then Rick Stubbs called again – attempting, as it turned out, to arrange Owen Clark's photo session.

'Please not now,' Mina said into the receiver.

Kip could hear Rick's voice twittering back at her.

'But he can change his flight,' she said.

More twittering.

'Can he do it here? In my room?' Kip knew that wouldn't be acceptable.

'Shit,' she said finally. 'I have to have ten minutes.' She tossed the phone back across the bed for Kip to replace in the handset.

'D'you want me to go?' he asked.

'No. What I want you to do, Kip, is go into the bathroom and bring me the bag you see there by the basin. And a glass of water.'

Kip fetched the bag and set it down with the water beside the phone. Mina heaved herself over to them, telling Kip to look away.

But he couldn't stop himself watching her pull a syringe and spoon out of the bag, together with a large brown bottle and some cotton wool. 'Are you shocked?' she asked, tapping some white powder from the bottle into the spoon.

'Of course not,' he lied.

'In America, this is called going uptown.'

'What does that mean?'

'You go uptown, it's cocaine. Downtown, it's smack. I went downtown, and now I go back uptown. Because your friend wants to take my picture.'

'I see,' said Kip, sitting on sweating palms.

She drew the dissolved coke through a tiny piece of cotton and tapped the syringe. Then she pulled up her sleeve.

Kip turned away, remembering Johnny Thunders at the party in Maida Vale. He heard Mina give a little cry as the coke hit her, and looked round to see blood trickling along the vein. An expression of bliss lit up her face.

'It's good stuff,' she said, shaking slightly. 'Not like the shit in London.' And then: 'You want some?'

'Oh, just a snort,' he shrugged.

Mina sprinkled the coke from the bottle, then flushed the syringe, spraying rose-coloured water on to the carpet. Kip rolled up a five-dollar note and snorted.

'Don't tell Rick I have this,' said Mina. 'Don't tell anyone or I'll kill you. You promise.'

'Absolutely,' said Kip, sniffing.

The Sacred Monsters had been rounded up by Stubbs and Spud and were awaiting Mina's arrival in the lobby. After the singer had come out of the lift with Kip, Owen shepherded the band into the street, heading towards a nearby scrapyard he'd earmarked for his location. Blinking in the mid-afternoon light, Kip walked behind the others with Mina.

They made a motley crew as Owen draped them across the auto wrecks. Kip got them down in his notebook: 'Dupont Greer, a black cowboy in a Stetson . . . Lee Krantz, an accountant on angel dust ... Jimmi Colena, missing link between John Travolta and Johnny Thunders ... Bo Hartman, suburban white Rasta ... and Mina herself.'

Before the band headed off for their soundcheck, Owen took some individual shots of Mina. Stoned though she was, she stood on the roof of a burned-out Chevrolet like some magnificent statue – cigarette in mouth, black-jeaned legs spread apart. There were wolf whistles from Jimmi and Dupont.

Onstage that night, there was something disjointed about the Sacred Monsters, and something hesitant about Mina herself. For the first time, Kip felt less than overawed. Krantz and Colena kept up a deafening barrage of sound, but it wasn't enough to save the show and Mina herself knew it. In the dressing room afterwards, she vented her rage on the band and the sound engineer, storming out of the theatre with Rick in hot pursuit.

Kip and Owen made their own way back to the Marriott, walking along Grand Avenue in the humid night air.

'What do you really think of Mina?' Kip asked.

'Well, it's not my kind of thing, is it? But I think she's interesting. Certainly bears out some of your Nietzschean theories.'

'It's funny, I almost doubted my own feelings tonight.' He paused for a second. 'Maybe I should come home with you tomorrow.'

'Why not? What are you gonna get out of her that you don't already know?'

'Right.'

'I mean, how far do you need to go?'

'You mean geographically or . . .'

'Or whatever.'

'Maybe the whole way.'

'Is that healthy?'

'What's "healthy"?'

They walked on.

EXTERMINATING ANGEL
On the Road with Mina and her
Monsters, Part One
by Kip Wilson
Junkyard portraits: Owen Clark

'the midnight souls who are brighter than
any day . . .

(Friedrich Nietzsche)

A house is not a motel, said Arthur Lee. But
then nor is a motel a house.

I don't know what I'm doing here, in another
cubicle, somewhere between Minneapolis and
Des Moines. This is 'life on the road', right?
The TV doesn't work and room service apears
to be on strike. My stomach hurts and I can't
sleep.

Owen Clark has gone home and now it's just
me and the Sacred Monsters of Desire, a
quartet of rock'n'roll mercenaries fronted by
ex-streetwalker Mina. You'll know by now that
she's the saviour of Western pop, etc. etc., and
that she's currently taking the US of A by
storm with this all-American band who cook
up an incendiary energy onstage, pushing her
to new heights – or should that be depths? – of
abandon.

Who'd have thought America would take
her to its breast? It was incredible enough that

we Brits saw the light so early and so clearly. Now your humble correspondent has to compete for her attention with old hippies from *Creem* and even glossy-mag harpies flown in from New York. All a bit galling, frankly.

We started out in Manhattan, witnessing a stupendous show at the Ritz. Hearing the Monsters reinterpret the likes of 'Ghost' and 'American Friend' instantly dispelled any misgivings about the junking of Mackaye and Salgado. Even more important, perhaps, the new material pointed onwards and upwards: 'Consumed' stung and 'Dead Zone' scorched, sweeping you up into heart-pounding exultation.

Watching Mina is like being under the thrall of some Aztec priestess commanding sacrifice. As she struts, glides, *convulses* her way around the stage, she makes old Susy Sue look frumpy, frankly. She's an exterminating angel, a cruel goddess whose will must be done. And with this whirlwind of noise behind her – this vortex of sound – she brooks no dissent. You'd happily follow her into the void of sonic bliss.

I suppose it's really quite simple. With a paltry handful of other acts past and present, Mina understands that music is a curse, a Faustian pact, a fatal intoxication. FIND YOURSELF IN EXTREME DANGER, enjoined the painter Jean Dubuffet, and Mina has seemingly taken such advice to heart. She walks the slenderest of tightropes across the existential abyss most of us choose to ignore, defying the void to swallow her up, taunting it with the unholy banshee shriek of her voice and the lewd splendour of her body.

Plato would have banned Mina from his republic, and with good reason – because she seeks to take music *beyond the pleasure principle*, beyond its workaday status of amusement, diversion, 'entertainment'. She knows that what music (at its most potent) intimates is the loss of identity itself. Like a drug, it blurs the boundaries we construct for ourselves as subjects in the humanist order.

So we hear disgruntled mutterings of drugs and 'decadence'. In the newly efficient, puritan-pop age, to risk this pact with the dark powers of rhythm and ritual is to be damned as retrogressive. No mystery, please, no whisper of the sickness at the core of the human heart. Summer's here and the time is right for shaking your booty in the street – with a little postmodernist twist, natch. Maybe Mina *is* retrogressive, but if she drags pop back to the days of 'Gimme Shelter', 'Sister Ray', Iggy's 'Dirt', that's fine by me. I'm not interested in your horrible Heaven 17s, your permed and preened Whams, I only want to hear from the ones who've CROSSED OVER INTO THE DARKNESS. So maybe the Strolling Crones blew it after *Exile*; maybe Iggy's blown it, too. But at least they descended briefly into the maelstrom of *jouissance*, of ecstatic self-destruction.

What the sniffy puritans fail to understand is that when you've descended as far into the maelstrom as Mina has, drugs are no longer recreational toys. How can you live with this knowledge *without* numbing and sedating yourself? After the degradation and humiliation of performance – a deranged exhibitionism in which Mina *becomes the sacrificial object* – only drugs can pull you back from 'the horror, the horror'.

Besides which, it's really none of their business.

The bus moves on through the heart of the mid-midwest. Colourless skies, endless logos rising up from the sides of freeways: Chevron, Days Inn, the ubiquitous 'M' of McDonalds. This isn't so much Nowheresville as Anywheresville. Everything is generic, little colonies replicating themselves endlessly. On the radio stations favoured by our driver, 'The Message' throbs its apocalyptic warning, sometimes segueing into Donna Summer's equally creepy 'Livin' In America'. Home of the brave, smell of the grave . . .

The Monsters are a motley crew, as you may already have gathered. You wonder how four such mismatched individuals ever pooled their talents in the first place. First there's 'lead' guitarist Lee Krantz, who could be an accountant from a distance but looks more unhinged the closer you get. Then there's 'rhythm' guitarist Jimmi Colena, would-be stud and missing link 'twixt John Travolta and Johnny Thunders. There's Dupont Greer, the black Dallas cowboy who 'just plays the bass and don't ask no questions'. And finally there's drummer Bo Hartman, a suburban white Rasta from Canada.

It's old Bo who looks the most approachable of the four, so during breakfast one morning I sit down next to him and ask what it's like to be a Sacred Monster.

'I like the room it gives me,' he says, a strip of bacon dangling from his mouth. 'Like, the band is real tight but I have a lotta scope just to go crazy. I know Dupont'll be there when I get back to the beat.'

Had you ever played with anyone like Mina before?

'The only thing I can compare it to is this old jazz cat I played with in Toronto. He was really into intensity – put his bands through the wringer every night.'

Are you surprised that Mina has built up such a cult following here?

'A little. The first time I listened to her album I was spooked by it, man. But the moment I played with her I knew we had something special here. Talk about intense.'

Do you think Mina is enjoying the tour?

'You'd have to ask *her* that. She certainly enjoyed the date in New York, but I don't know about Pittsburgh.'

I get less out of bassman Greer, who smokes menthol cigarettes and claims he's none too clear what Mina is even singing about. 'But hell, I'd rather be behind Mina than Freddie King. No offence, Freddie, but when it come to fishnet stockings there ain't no contest.'

As for Colena, a more Neanderthal attitude towards the fairer sex it would be hard to find, even in Brooklyn. 'My first impression was that she was *a fox*!' he exclaims, adding that it's a good thing he plays the guitar. 'I get so turned on sometimes I have to thank the Lord for making me a guitar player, if you know what I mean.'

Whereas if you were a flautist . . .

'A what?'

Oh dear, Jimmi probably thinks a flute is some sex toy. Well, thanks anyway, Jimmi.

'You got it, man! Be sure and give my love to London.'

Lee Krantz is a rather different kettle of fish, a man with some sign of mental life beyond the basic level of appetite. At the same time, he's the prickliest and most guarded of the Monsters, prone to saying things like: 'Rock music is just a day job I happen to do at night', and 'Metal is a dead concept in 1982'. He sits on the bus in his button-down shirts and you wonder how he came to pick up an electric guitar at all.

'I have various musical outlets,' says Krantz 'all of them concerned with extending the boundaries of sonic terrorism. Mina appealed to me first because I am interested in the figure of the deranged diva, and second because she brings a Germanic aesthetic to bear on American rock.'

You've written most of the new songs together.

'It's a new thing for me to collaborate on something as formal as "Consumed". I quite surprised myself by enjoying the process.'

What's Mina like to work with?

'Always very clear about what she wants.'

How much has she been influenced by the kind of 'No Wave' bands in which you've played?

'For me, the term "No Wave" is as redundant as the term "New Wave", so I'm not sure what you're talking about.'

Well, Mars, DNA, Teenage Jesus . . .

'I never played in those bands.'

Well, to your knowledge, did they have any influence on the Monsters' sound?

'I doubt it very much. This is a very different thing we have here. You've got to understand that Jimmi or Dupont wouldn't even know who you're talking about.'

How are you finding the shows?

'Very interesting for the most part. Mina has something I haven't seen in many female American performers, which is a sort of pure demonic rage. Also, she doesn't have what I would call a rock voice, so I enjoy her singing every night.'

Is *she* enjoying it?

'"Enjoyment" is perhaps not a word I would attach to Mina. But I think she's amused by America, and you could describe that as enjoyment.'

Andy Warhol said the glamour of his stars was 'rooted in despair'. It's that kind of 'glamour' we see in Mina, who occasionally brings to mind the young Nico – and let's not forget the mighty 'Evening of Light', after all.

Mina stares at America through dark shades and sea-green bus windows. Although buoyed by the power of the Sacred Monsters' shows, she already seems weary of the rigmaroles of touring. Asked about her burgeoning cult success Stateside, she shrugs her shoulders, at a loss to explain why *La Ronde* is selling so well.

'Perhaps Joan Jett has failed to satisfy America fully,' she ventures finally, a Mona Lisa smile playing across her lips.

How have you adjusted to life without the sidemen who played such a big part in *La Ronde*?

'I think you can see I have adjusted with no problem. It's very different, of course, but better for me. I miss some things they did, but this band is the right thing now.'

Why did you part company with Mackaye and Salgado?

'They did not want to go in this direction. They wanted to go back into jazz. I am still talking with them, it's no big deal.'

How have you found writing with a new partner?

'We wrote in New York before rehearsing for the tour, and the songs came very well. "Consumed", "Art Of Darkness", "Isabel", "Dead Zone". All of these I am happy about. It's nothing like writing with Dave or Boris. The songs are bigger, more American.'

Is it depressing touring America and realising most people just want the old clichés reprocessed – like Joan Jett?

'No, it's good that the mainstream is always like Joan Jett. It helps me to understand what I am doing.'

Tell me why you're a performer.

'I cannot say. This was never my dream or my goal. It was just the logical thing to do after being a prostitute.'

Artaud said theatre should be 'a terrible and dangerous act – the real organic and physical transformation of the human body'. Are you transformed in performance?

'When I am on the stage, my body is something to be used, even abused. I touch myself,

I hurt myself, I lose my shame. So maybe there is a transformation.'

Would you go as far as Jim Morrison, who was so inspired by the Living Theatre's idea of violence and obscenity that he exposed himself onstage?

'See, it is not a contest to see *how far you can go*. It is not to shock people for the sake of shock. For me, it is natural to go to the extreme, or sometimes not. Sometimes I do not go to the edge because there is no point.'

What are your impressions of America so far?

'You want me to say it is not like in the movies? Well, it is not like in the movies!'

Do you like it?

'It's fine. Everything is convenient. Everything that you want is in front of you.'

What about Americans?

'They are honest, they have no pretence. In Europe and England, nobody says how they really feel.'

Could you live here?

'Maybe.'

Even *here*, in the middle of nowhere?

'Sure.'

Are you happy at the moment?

'What is "happy"? Happy is not relevant. I make music because I have to do something with my life, not because I am some artist expressing myself. I can't live normally, so I live as an object. People watch me, they listen to me sing. When I perform, I exist.'

Where do you see yourself in ten years?

'I *don't* see myself in ten years.'

Do you think you'll still be making music?

'No.'

Why not?

'Because it won't work for me any more.'

Would you ever go into films or something like that?

'Well, Fassbinder is dead, so . . .'

You like Fassbinder?

'Very much.'

Is there a part of you that's still very Austrian/German?

'Of course. Sometimes if I watch Fassbinder's films it makes me want to go home.'

Do you have any contact with your family?

'No, I don't know where they are.'

Do you prefer to feel rootless in the world, without attachments?

'Yes.'

What about love?

'What about it?'

Have you had any lasting relationships?

'Only with pimps.'

Who are your heroes?

'I have no heroes. You want me to say Piaf, Brel, Billie Holiday? I have, how you say, *affinities* with some singers and writers. No heroes.'

Are you still bothered by the drug rumours that follow you around?

'I never was bothered by them. People can think what they like. I'm sorry for them that they cannot find something more interesting to talk about.'

Could 'Dead Zone' in any way be construed as a drug song?

'Is it a drug song? It could be. But it could be about many things, not just drugs.'

Do you think drugs have inspired great songs?

'Yes, but also some really stupid songs. Like what is that one – "Golden Brown"?! Pah!'

Stomachs are rumbling, so the bus pulls off Interstate 35 for some nosh. Mina stubs out her cigarette and prepares for another encounter with middle America. Her manager Rick Stubbs gives me a slap on the back, asks how the interview went. We disembark, ready to fill our faces. Jimmi Colena is already eyeing up some Prairie Rose of a waitress, and Dupont Greer is nudging him in the ribs. It's all a world away from the Europe of *La Ronde*.

Sitting at yet another corner table, her eyes concealed behind another pair of sunglasses, Mina could almost be The Woman Who Fell To Earth. One dare not ask the nature of her mission.

15

Kip had put the finishing touches to 'Exterminating Angel', the first of the two on-the-road reports on the Sacred Monsters' tour, and was lying wide awake in his Quality Inn bed. It was 2.30 in the morning.

Thoughts of Mina tormented him as he lay in the darkness. He saw again the trickle of blood along her arm, her head thrown back and her mouth open. He remembered her in a bathrobe in New York, how he'd almost seen her breasts. Now he thought of her two floors above, maybe sleeping, maybe shooting up again.

He wondered whether he should have flown home with Owen Clark.

He knew at 3 o'clock that sleep wouldn't come, so he semi-dressed and set off for a walk he hoped might tire him out. He thought about walking to a nearby 7–11, but instead found himself taking a lift to the fourth floor, where Mina was sleeping. The lift stopped and he got out, turning left towards room 414.

As he approached the room, he saw that the door was very slightly ajar. Through the crack, moreover, he could hear muffled voices and the faint sound of a guitar. When he dared to peek into the room he saw Jimmi Colena, shirtless, with a jumbo acoustic on which he was strumming Led Zeppelin's 'Goin' To California'.

Behind Jimmi, in the bed, lay Mina and another girl, both apparently naked. The girl, dark haired, couldn't have been more than sixteen or seventeen and was pretty in a wholesome American way. She was also very obviously stoned, and began accompanying Jimmi in a tuneless voice. Mina, meanwhile, had propped herself up with some pillows and was drinking from a tumbler. There were bottles and cans on the floor.

Kip stood at the door, hardly daring to breathe. He was sure that if he retreated he would be heard.

Suddenly Jimmi stopped playing and all three of them were looking towards the door.

'Who's there?' asked Mina.

Kip thought about turning back towards the lift but saw that he was trapped. He pushed open the door and stuttered an apology.

'My God, it's you!' said Mina.

'The midnight rambler,' added Jimmi Colena.

'What are you doing here?' Mina asked.

'I – I couldn't sleep. I was just walking, and . . .' He tried not to look at her.

'You walk past my door in the middle of the night.'

'Yes. I mean – '

'Sure you ain't one o' them *peepers*?' asked Jimmi. 'You English are all perverts.'

'No, I . . .'

'You like what you see?' Jimmi asked.

'I – '

'Listen, why don't you siddown, have a drink?' Jimmi motioned towards a chair. 'Oh, and meet Shari . . .'

Kip nodded awkwardly at the girl in the bed, then sat

down. 'I – ,' he tried again, but Jimmi cut him off with another guitar chord. He concealed his embarrassment by opening a bottle of vodka and pouring some into a glass.

While Jimmi sang David Bowie's 'Rock and Roll Suicide', the dark-haired girl leaned over towards Mina and began kissing her on the mouth. Kip watched them through his glass as he drank.

'You wanna join in, Mr Rock Journalist?' asked Jimmi without breaking off from the song.

'I think I'd better go,' Kip said as he got to his feet.

'Aw, come on,' said Jimmi. Kip could see that Shari had her left hand on Mina's right breast.

Suddenly Kip caught Mina's eye as the girl began kissing her breasts. He saw only frozen indifference in her gaze, and looked away. In a state approaching shock, he put down his glass and walked hurriedly out of the room.

The sound of laughter followed him down the corridor.

A veritable media circus greeted the Sacred Monsters in Los Angeles. The 'buzz' on Mina had travelled all the way to Tinseltown, and a horde of scribes and scenesters were waiting to press her flesh at the Sunset Marquis. Kip slunk into the foyer of the hotel behind the band as Rick Stubbs barked orders and buttered up some Warner Brothers executives who were lunching by the pool.

There had been no mention of Kip's humiliating experience at the Quality Inn. He'd felt so groggy and disorientated the next morning that he wondered if he hadn't dreamt the whole thing. On the flight to LA he avoided eye contact with Mina and Jimmi and buried himself in an old copy of *Rolling Stone*.

From his room, he looked out at a hot, smoggy sky. He felt a new sense of expendability, as though he'd outlasted his own usefulness to the Rick Stubbs masterplan. But there was one more piece to write for *Cover*, live from Hollywood Babylon, and Rick had said he could interview Mina after the two Roxy shows that night.

There was half a day to kill in Hollywood, so Kip decided to go for a walk. As he headed east along Sunset in the bleached, hazy light, 'Ghost' played on some infernal jukebox in his head and images of Mina's body seemed to coil around him. Gibbering bums passed him on the street; bewigged lunatics raved at the traffic.

Forty minutes later he turned left on north Cahuenga and walked up to the motel where he and Mark Oliver had been ransacked by T-man. He remembered Venice Beach and the Stars' Homes tour, heard again the punk tapes they'd brought with them. A sense of sadness came over him as he thought how that American holiday had all but finished their friendship.

Taking a different route back to the Sunset Marquis, he was stopped in his tracks by the sight of a prostitute fellating some overweight slob in an Oldsmobile. With a mixture of fascination and repulsion, he watched her head bobbing up and down in his lap. Walking on, the memory of Shari's hand on Mina's breast came back to him like some repressed primal scene.

The queue for the first Roxy show stretched almost the whole way round the block. As he walked past them with Spud, Kip was surprised to see that Mina's fans comprised members of every southern Californian species: punks, Goths, New Romantics with Flock of Seagulls hair sculptures. Inside, meanwhile, Warner Brothers appeared to have sent half their staff down to check out what one Hawaiian-shirted A&R man called the 'Scary Monsters'.

Backstage, Mina was haranguing Rick Stubbs for another of his 'oversights' when Jimmi Colena came into the room, a Fender Telecaster swinging from his hip.

'Someone said Teddy Templeman's here,' Jimmi reported.

'Oh, they're all here,' said Rick.

'So whaddya think of LA, man?'

Kip looked up and realised Jimmi was addressing him. 'Um, it's OK,' he said hurriedly. To his amazement, the guitarist then sat down with an evil leer on his face and played the chords to 'Going To California'.

'Can that shit and find me a tuner,' said Dupont Greer, who'd walked in wearing a new white Stetson.

'Dupont, you look like a goddam pimp,' said Jimmi.

'I *is* a goddam pimp, you guinea fuck,' Dupont replied. 'I got me some fine bitches here on Sunset Boooolivaarrd.'

'Dupont, you buck-nigger motherfuck, do me a favour and hit that root note on 'Dead Zone' tonight. You're always losing me when you go off on that dumb walking riff of yours.'

'Well, pardon me, Mr James Co-Lena or whatever your name be. What kinda name is that anyways? Sound like a motherfucking in-tes-tine.'

'Well, excuuuuuuse me, Mr, uh, *Dupont* fuckin' Greer. I forgot you had such a cool goddam name yourself.'

Mina had been making herself up in the corner, apparently oblivious to this banter, but now she was swivelling round to ask for some quiet. 'Why do you Americans always have to talk like you were in a bad movie?' she asked.

'Baby, you in Hollywood now,' said Dupont.

A panting Rick Stubbs re-entered the room. 'Half an hour,' he said breathlessly. 'It is *electric* out there.'

Lee Krantz wore a checked lumberjack shirt and black jeans, Hartman a curious silver jump suit. 'What kind of rider do they call this?' asked Bo, poking at a sandwich. 'Gimme a beer, Jimmi.'

Colena hurled him a Coors. 'Don't go too wild tonight, huh, Bo?' he said. 'Sometimes, man, I don't know where the hell I am with you.'

'But that's the whole point, Jimbo. Live dangerously. Live bebop.'

'This ain't bebop, Mr Jump-Suit Drummer Man. You gotta carry the beat or the rest of us are fucked.'

Rick wandered over to Mina. 'You hadn't forgotten you're talking to Kip tonight,' he said.

'How could I forget?' she replied without looking round.

Mina was as spellbinding that night as she'd ever been. While Bo bashed out a Mo Tucker stomp and Lee delivered the sten-gun guitar riff of 'Poison Doll', she floated on to the stage in a cloud of smoke, her hair tucked into a black beret. On 'Ugly', she dropped to her knees and mimed fellatio with her mic, all the while screaming into it. 'We have now our heavy metal medley,' she said in the set's only spoken intro. The band instantly launched into 'Art Of Darkness', followed by a snatch of 'War Pigs' and a revamped 'Evening Of Light'. By the last of these, the beret had come off and Mina's hair was whirling about her head. The whole club seemed caught up in the trance-like drone of the song, which throbbed on as she shook herself into a state of near ecstasy. Finally she tore off her jacket, hurling it back over Dupont's amplifier.

There were yelps and whistles as Krantz chopped out the riff from 'American Friend'. Kip wondered how many of these Americans understood what the song was about. If they were in any doubt, Mina had decided to spell it out for them, leaning back against the bass amp as the song built to its feverish climax and pushing her mic against her crotch. The effect was crude but riveting. Kip trembled as she repeatedly jammed the bulbous mic head between her legs, her screams all the more harrowing for being barely audible. She followed the song with 'The Death Of Desire', sung in an icy monotone to the starkest accompaniment: just Krantz scratching at his guitar and Bo smashing his cymbals. This led finally into 'Bitter-Sweet', prompting shouts of recognition from a rather camp contingent of fans at Mina's feet.

Responding to roars of approval from the audience, the Sacred Monsters played two encores, beginning with the anguished 'Ghost' and finishing with a sweeping, delirious 'European Nights'. The latter went down a treat with the group at Mina's feet, for whom she appeared to be an icon of tragic European glamour. As the set ended, Kip made his way out of the Roxy and walked along Sunset to the hotel. Already a large crowd was gathering on the sidewalk for the second show.

Three hours passed before the phone rang in Kip's room. He started from semi-sleep and heard Rick telling him to be in Mina's room in fifteen minutes. Splashing water on his face, he tried desperately to think of some questions to ask. He remembered sitting in Sid's before that first interview, and wished Stevie was with him now.

'Hi, how was the second show?' he blurted nervously as she opened the door in a Sunset Marquis bathrobe. He was relieved to see no sign of Jimmi Colena in the room.

'Not bad,' she said. 'Not the best.'

She walked over to the minibar, asking if he wanted a drink.

'Please,' he said. He added that the Sunset Marquis made a pleasant change after the motels they'd slept in.

'Yeah, but it's full of rock groups,' she said with a smile, emptying two miniatures into a glass. 'You go home tomorrow?'

'Yes.'

'So how have you enjoyed your week with the Sacred Monsters Of Desire?'

'It's been quite an experience, I suppose.'

'Is that all?'

'What do you want me to say?'

'From *you* I expect more.'

Kip looked down at his beer.

'Tell me, were you shocked by what you saw last night? Or are you used to that?'

'Not *shocked*, of course not . . .'

'You sure you weren't spying on me, Kip?'

'No, I wasn't spying on you.'

'I'm not stupid, you know. I know how you look at me.' She walked to the bathroom and brought back the washbag he remembered from Chicago. 'Tonight we celebrate your last night,' she said as she sat down beside him.

'You trying to shock me again?' Kip managed to say with a half smile. But there was no reply as she set to work preparing a fix of heroin and cocaine. 'Now we go uptown *and* downtown,' she said finally.

'*We* go?'

'You don't want to come?'

'Um, not for me, thanks.'

'Now now, you have to take your medicine.'

'Can't I just – '

'Don't worry, little boy, you won't feel a thing.'

Soon she'd cooked the heroin and was tapping coke into the spoon.

'I can't believe this is happening,' he said as Mina rolled up his sleeve. Moments later he felt the prick of the needle and begged her to stop. But it was too late, for a warm wave was rolling through his thighs and his brain was exploding in a flash of white light.

Mina smiled, spraying Kip's diluted blood into a glass. The coke rush died away and left only the warm, sickly undertow of heroin. Staring at himself in the bathroom mirror, Kip imagined his mother watching them.

When he came back into the bedroom, Mina was preparing to shoot up in her foot. 'Why there?' he asked.

'Rick said he saw my tracks onstage,' she replied, her brow furrowed by the concentration the operation entailed. Soon there was a sweet sigh of relief as she sank back in the chair. He sat on the edge of the bed and watched her.

At last she opened her eyes.

'Kip, you care something about me, no?' she said. 'You can say.' And somehow it was all right for him to say that yes, he did care about her.

She moved towards him from the chair, her bathrobe slipping off her shoulders as he stared up at her.

'Can you lie back?' she asked. He did as she said.

Slowly she climbed along his body until her sex was over his face.

'Play with yourself,' she asked as she looked down at him. While he unzipped his fly, she lowered herself over his mouth and began to grind herself into his face, pushing her cunt over his mouth and nose and making a noise like a loud sob as she rose to orgasm. He jerked himself frenziedly, the taste of sweet shit in his mouth as she came.

Raising herself off him, Mina reached down to undo his belt. Quickly, she pulled his jeans along his legs. Then he was watching her walk back to the table to snort some coke.

Suddenly, Mina took something out of her washbag.

'What are you doing?' said Kip in disbelief as he saw the belted dildo she was fastening round her waist.

'Turn over, Kip,' she said as she walked back to the bed.

He turned and felt her fingers lubricating his asshole. 'Please, Mina . . .'

Her breasts flattened against his back as the dildo entered his ass. Slowly, she pushed it deep into him, reaching under him as the pain became unendurable.

'Oh Kip,' she said, masturbating him.

He came into her hand, the jizz spitting out of him like vomit. 'Yes, little boy,' she whispered in his ear.

There was one final stab of pain as she withdrew.

16

Dez Frippett had only got a little way into 'The Scary Monstrosity Of Desire' – part two of Kip's Mina feature – when he realised the boy had gone 'way over the edge'.

It was the phrase he used when Joe Grout poked his head round the door one afternoon in September.

'Always did think he was a bit strange', said Joe.

'No, but this is really doolally. I hate to think what the guy's *on*.'

'Let's have a look,' said Joe. Dez passed him the piece, which must have been seven thousand words long.

Joe perused the opening paragraph, then flipped forward at random. 'Jesus, the guy's obsessed with sex. I mean, what *is* this? "Rock is itself an act of penetration, as Iggy knew, and as all of us who've allowed it to ravish us must acknowledge . . ."?! And then, "Mina castrates the clichés of male rock, chopping America's cock off . . ."!!'

'Good one that.'

'Maybe you should ask Ava about him. He must be a total perv.'

'He's supposed to come in this afternoon. Christ knows what I'm going to say.'

Ava Cadaver was the first person to spot Kip as he crept in. She gave a slight start at his appearance, since most of his hair had been shorn off and he looked thin to the point of emaciation.

'Kip, my God,' she said, pausing in the middle of her piece on the Lords of the New Church.

'Oh hi,' he said, though he looked straight through her.

'How did it all go?' she asked.

'Amazing, Ava, amazing.'

'So what's with the haircut?'

'Oh, you know . . . change of image?'

'You can say that again. Who cut it, if you don't mind me asking?'

'I did, actually. Does it look awful?'

'It looks a bit odd.'

'Well, saved me a bit of money.'

'Right.'

There was an awkward silence. Ava said Dez wanted a word with him.

'About my piece?'

'I guess.'

Kip had spent over a week writing and rewriting 'The Scary Monstrosity of Desire', determined that it should be a triumphant summation of all his ideas and theories about Mina. His central thesis was that she was a 'phrophet of despair', a woman who understood that the sole *raison d'être* left to man in the late twentieth century lay in evil. Mina, he argued, saw that beneath the veneer of good will in Western society lurked a profound malevolence. He was bolstered in this notion by his reading of the Marquis de Sade's *The 120 Days of Sodom*.

So pleased was he with the finished result – an epic tract the like of which had never been seen in *Cover* – that it came as something of a jolt to see the mildly distressed look on Dez's face as he sat down for what the editor called 'a little chat about things'.

'First off, Kip, thanks for turning it round so fast,' Dez began.

'My pleasure, Dez.'

'On the other hand, the piece is . . .' He gave a nervous laugh. 'Well, what can I say? It's not your standard rock feature, is it now? Just in terms of length it's pretty extreme.'

'I can make cuts.'

'But that's not the whole problem, is it? I mean, it's wacky stuff, Kip! What the hell were you on when you wrote this?'

'I wasn't on anything.'

'Really?'

'What d'you mean by "wacky"?'

'I mean basically that you use Mina as a platform for launching all kinds of frankly disturbing ideas while barely mentioning her music or anything our readers might actually wish to read about. I'm not saying you're the first *Cover* writer ever to do this, but you really take the prize for sheer self-indulgence.'

'Self-*indulgence*?'

'Call it what you like, but that's what it is.'

'Oh, come on.'

'Look, the simple fact is that I can't use this piece as it stands. I can't *begin* to think of using it.'

'You're not serious.'

'On the level, mate. I want you to go back to the drawing board and start again. This time bearing your readers in mind, not all of whom fancy themselves as Ronald Barts.'

Kip looked at his shoes. In a somewhat faltering voice, he said he might have to take the piece somewhere else.

Dez tried not to laugh. 'Really, I think you'd have a hard job getting anyone else to publish this,' he said. 'Fact is, I give people like you more elbow room that most editors would.' He paused. 'Look, there's no need to go storming off in a huff. Apart from anything else, we've just sent you to America for ten days and we've got to have something to show for that.'

'You're not going to pretend you paid for the plane tickets and hotel rooms.'

'No, but . . .'

'Well, you can fuck off then.'

Ava looked up anxiously as Dez's door slammed shut. Kip was apparently making for the lifts.

'What happened?' she called out.

'I'm not writing another word for this paper,' he replied without looking round. Heads turned towards him.

Ava got up from her desk and ran out after him. 'You serious?' she asked as they waited for the lift.

'My piece obviously went way over his sad suburban head, so he's not going to use it.'

'He wants a rewrite?'

'He's not going to get it.'

'Well, hold on.'

'Look, I won't compromise on this, just because he personally can't handle it.'

'Kip, there's no guarantee someone else'll take it. There's no guarantee anyone will even give you work.'

'That's what he said. He tries to make out like he's the only editor in London who's prepared to take risks, which is crap.'

'Where are you going?' she asked, following him into the lift.

'Fuck knows.'

'You wanna coffee?'

They picked a café not normally patronised by *Cover* hacks.

'Listen, I haven't read the piece,' Ava said as they sat down at a corner table. 'But . . .'

'But what?'

'But Dez wouldn't be saying this without good reason. Maybe you should calm down and look at things objectively. Maybe you're too close to your subject here.'

'But the whole point is to *get close to your subject*. Who needs more bland fucking objectivity?'

'I guess Dez does.'

'Well, fuck him.'

'Sometimes you just have to compromise, Kip.'

'I don't accept that people wouldn't understand this piece, and it's fucking arrogant of Dez Frippett to assume his readers lack the grey matter to do so.'

They sat in silence for a moment.

'Tell me, what did Mina do to you?' Ava asked suddenly.

'I'm sorry?' said Kip, startled by the question.

'She did something to you, didn't she? I mean, fucked with your head in some way.'

'Is that what you think?'

'Yeah, it is what I think.'

There was a further pause as Kip stared into his coffee. For a second he thought he was going to cry.

'You wanna talk about it?' asked Ava.

'Maybe she did "fuck with my head",' he said finally.

'What happened?'

'It's . . . difficult to describe. D'you have a cigarette?'

'You don't smoke.'

'I do now.'

She passed him a cigarette and lit it. 'What happened?'

He drew in a lungful of smoke and instantly felt better. 'She just led me on, that's all. Broke my poor little heart.'

'I don't believe you.'

'God's truth.'

Ava watched him and said nothing.

Stevie put his monthly stockcheck on hold when, late in the afternoon, he observed Ava Cadaver coming through the door of Vinyl Dementia.

'If it isn't the Queen of Darkness herself,' he said. 'And to what do we owe this honour?'

'Listen, I know we're not the best of friends,' Ava replied, 'but I've come to ask you about Kip.'

'What about Kip?'

'Has he told you anything about what happened in America with Mina?'

'What did happen?'

'I don't know. Something.'

'He did sort of hint that something went on. But then he clammed up about it.'

'Yeah, you see, I got the feeling he wanted to tell me something but for some reason he couldn't, or it wouldn't come out.'

'You could be right.'

'It's almost like he's traumatised.'

'She's a strange one, that's for sure.'

'She's a sick bitch is what she is.'

'You care about him, don't yer?'

'Tell me something, have *you* ever slept with Kip?'

'You what?!'

'Have you?'

'Don't make us laugh, love!'

'I just wondered.'

After Stevie had shut up the shop, he and Ava walked slowly up the Portobello Road to Notting Hill Gate. It gave them more time to compare notes on the subject of Kip Wilson.

'See, the thing about Kip is he's middle-class to the tips of his toes,' said Stevie. 'Grew up in a vicarage, went to public school, all that malarkey. Parents teach, sister's at Cambridge. You're talking about this dreamy little boy who discovered pop music when he was twelve and sort of dropped out of the real world. He's still that little dreamer at the back of the classroom.'

'What sort of girlfriends did he have?' Ava asked.

'Didn't really have any. There was Julie, of course, she was the reason we got talking in the first place. But that was about it.'

'I think I saw her once.'

'Yeah? Well, he really lost it over 'er. But then he clapped eyes on Mina. And you, of course.'

'The thing is, she *is* very beautiful.'

'If you like 'em like that.'

'But . . .'

'But there's sommat a bit fuckin' warped about the whole thing.'

'Yes.'

When they'd turned on to Notting Hill Gate, Stevie stopped beneath the underground sign to say goodbye. 'Let's get him committed,' he laughed.

Ava laughed with him but a part of her wanted to cry.

BEST OF '82: KIP WILSON

1 *Consumed* (EP) – Sacred Monsters of Desire
2 *La Ronde* (LP) – Mina
3 *Bach's Bottom* (compliation) – Alex Chilton
4 'Living In America' (single) – Donna Summer
5 *Damaged* (LP) – Black Flag
6 'Wild Women With Steak-Knives' (track) – Diamanda Galas
7 *Sulk* (LP) – Associates
8 'Junkyard' (track) – Birthday Party
9 *Inflatable Boy Clams* (EP)
10 'The Message' (single) – Grandmaster Flash & Furious Five
11 'Faithless' (single) – Scritti Politti
12 *Meat Puppets* (LP)
13 'Desire' (track) – Malaria
14 *Liaisons Dangereuses* (LP)
15 'Say Hello, Wave Goodbye' (single) – Soft Cell

Evening Standard, January 4th, 1983

SINGER TO UNDERGO TREATMENT FOR DRUGS

Austrian-born rock star Mina yesterday arrived at an exclusive West Country clinic to begin treatment for drug addiction. The singer, whose group the Sacred Monsters of Desire recently had a Top 20 American hit with 'Consumed', declined to comment on her problems.

A spokesman for the group said Mina had begun using drugs to cope with the stress of touring last year. He added that the Sacred Monsters would begin work on a new album as soon as Mina had completed treatment. 'She is exhausted at the moment and has decided to sort herself out before continuing with the group,' he said.

17

When Kip called Spearhead Management, the familiar mid-Atlantic tones of Rick Stubbs came on the line almost immediately. 'Kip, if you're calling about *her*, I no longer represent her.'

'Sorry?'

'You heard me. She's *let go* of me, my friend. And that's a very polite way of putting it.'

'When?'

'About ten days ago.'

'Gosh.'

'Yep, the crazy bitch has gone. I should be grateful, really.'

'Is it true she's gone into a clinic?'

'Depends if you believe what they write in the papers, Kip.'

'You don't happen to know the name of it.'

'Why? You working for *The Sun*?'

'No reason, really.'

'Something Lodge . . . Wickham Lodge.'

'Thanks, Rick. Sorry to bother you.'

'*De nada*, amigo. So long.'

There was a tap on Kip's shoulder, and he gave a start.

'How was yer Christmas, pet?' asked Stevie.

'Who the fuck let *you* in?' said Kip. 'And don't sneak up on me like that!'

'S'pose I should've made an appointment or sommat.'

'Do you want to go out for a drink?'

'Only if you have the time, your lordship.'

In a chintzy Paddington pub, Kip told Stevie the news about Mina.

'Oh, not her again,' his friend sighed.

'Well, don't you think it's an interesting twist to the tale?'

'Look, I'm not gonna wag me finger at yer, but personally I think you should stay well away.'

'Did I say I was going to see her? I'm not going to see her.'

'Good.'

'But I can't suddenly pretend she doesn't interest me.'

'She's a fucked-up kraut with a smack problem. How interesting is that?'

'Shall we change the subject?'

Ava rang from *Cover* to ask if Kip wanted to see a movie with her and Stevie. He said he didn't know. She said that Malcolm Reeves, who'd recently taken over from Pamela Motown as *Cover*'s live reviews editor, wanted to know where Kip's John Cale review was. 'Have you actually written it yet?' she asked.

'Sort of.'

'What does "sort of" mean?'

'Let's just say it's on the tip of my mind.'

She sighed.

'Maybe you and Stevie should see the movie on your own,' said Kip. 'It's ironic that you two are getting on so famously now.'

'You wanna see the film or not?'

'What is it?'

'*The Battle of Algiers*.'

'Where and when?'

'Russell Square at seven thirty.'

'Well, all right.'

At least he's not late, Ava thought as Kip shuffled towards her in an outsize sweater.

'What happened to the coat?' she asked.

'It died.'

'Shame.'

'Well, it had a good innings.'

'You warm enough?'

'Not if Stevie keeps us waiting.'

The failure of their relationship seemed to hang in the cold air around them.

'Any excitement in the office today?' he asked.

'Not really. Only the rumours that Dez is being kicked upstairs.'

'You serious?'

'Yep.'

'Who'll they get to replace him?'

'The word is Joe Grout or Dave Duncan.'

'You've got to be joking.'

'Quite. I reckon they'll bring in someone from outside.'

As she spoke, Stevie sauntered towards them, a beret placed at a jaunty angle on his head. 'Hello, darlings,' he chirped like a Scouse Noël Coward.

They bought tickets and banana bread, and Kip sat between Ava and Stevie. As they watched the scenes of resistance fighters scurrying down flights of steps and bolting through alleyways, Stevie giggled in Kip's ear. 'Always did like north Africans,' he said.

The usual desultory post-movie reflections kept the talk flowing on the tube ride to Leicester Square. If Kip had been honest he'd have said the most remarkable thing about *The Battle of Algiers* was that it stopped him thinking about Mina for minutes at a time. But then that might have been playing into the hands of these friends whom he suspected in any case of having ulterior motives for arranging this rendezvous. He kept waiting for the telltale note of confrontation, and it duly came as they sat down in the Italian restaurant on Old Compton Street.

'So, Kip,' said Stevie, chewing on a piece of *ciabatta*.

'So, Stevie.'

'Whatcha working on at the moment?'

'Not a lot.'

'*Cover* not giving you much to do?'

'No. I just don't feel like writing.'

'Not even about Mina?'

'Not even about Mina.'

'Listen, what happened when you were in America? What did that nutty bird do to yer?'

'"Nutty bird"! Jesus, you are so small minded . . .'

'That's priceless from you!'

Ava repeated Stevie's question.

'Ava, what do you *think* happened? You think I did smack with her? Screwed her? What?'

'*I don't know*, Kip. I wish I knew.'

'Nothing happened. *Nothing*.'

A waitress came to the table and asked if they were ready to order. Kip glanced at his menu but he knew that he wasn't going to eat.

Stevie asked the waitress to come back later and turned again to his friend. 'Look, Kip, we ain't trying to attack you, we just care about you. Somebody's gotta say something.'

'I could say mind your own fucking business.'

'So what are friends for if they can't tell you when you're going off the rails?'

Kip stared for a moment at his menu. Then he rose to his feet.

'You're right, Stephen,' he said. 'What *are* friends for?'

Ava and Stevie watched him turn and walk fast out of the restaurant.

20th Jan., 1983

Dear Mina,

Please forgive me for writing to you like this. When I read that you were going into the clinic, I couldn't help thinking about you and hoping you were OK. I hope you aren't in too much pain.

Obviously we haven't spoken since that last night in LA, which now seems like a long time ago. You may have wondered whatever happened to part two of my piece about the tour. As it happens, I did write it, but the editor of *Cover* claimed his precious readers wouldn't understand it. Perhaps I should send you a copy.

I want you to know that I think often about you. I would love to see you again, just to talk things over.

Yours,

Kip

Wickham Lodge,
nr. Bath

February 27

Dear Kip,

I am feeling bad about what happened in America. I did not mean to hurt you, but the drugs did bad things to me. I was full of cruelty and sickness, you were my victim.

Probably it's best you don't send me what you wrote about the Sacred Monsters. That is all behind me, I cannot turn back.

Kip, I must ask you a favour. I am ashamed of what I did to you, but please understand I cannot see you. I have to cut off my past to begin again. Try to forget me and my music. I thank you for being my champion at the start but now it is better that you move on.

I ask you not to write to me again, and I hope you will understand why I say it.

Mina.

18

A month after he'd received it, Mina's letter was still in Kip's bedside drawer at the vicarage. Often during the day he would take it out and read it, pretending to himself that it was a kind of coded love letter.

He remembered how he'd collapsed when he'd first read it. He'd tried to find out whether Mina was still in residence at Wickham Lodge, only to be told that they didn't disclose any information about their patients.

In despair, finally, he called *Cover* to ask Don Barstow if there was any more news about Mina. Don took two days to return the call, but sounded mightily amused when he did. Mina, he said, had not only left the clinic but was planning to record a Christian rock album. 'Maybe she'll do a duet with Cliff Richard,' he tittered.

Life in the vicarage was bearable only because Kip could stay in his bedroom. Outside the room there was always the threat of Gemma, who'd just terminated her studies at Cambridge in order to put a large chunk of England between her and Jeremy Bagshaw. Even Sheila Wilson, bustling about the house in a frenzy of dusting and polishing, was to be avoided now. Kip computed that the minimum he could get away with was a spot of washing up and the occasional exercise of Sheila's overweight labrador Winnie. He could often be seen plodding across the neighbouring fields with a Walkman on, Winnie bringing up the rear with no little difficulty.

Housework was the only thing that stopped Sheila worrying about her children; Michael Wilson was certainly no help in the matter. Supper at the vicarage was generally a joyless affair, enlivened only by the odd tantrum. Sheila talked about Winnie, Gemma about prospective suitors. Michael periodically asked someone to pass him the salt.

When it all became too depressing, Kip returned to his room, where he would pull Mina's letter out of its drawer. He'd started a reply to her at least five times but abandoned it on each occasion, afraid of blowing any chance of seeing her again.

From time to time he wondered what Stevie and Ava were up to, but his pride was too great for him to make any move towards a *rapprochement*. When he remembered their little confrontation in Soho – their misconceived attempt at an 'intervention' – he felt only rage.

Several weeks passed before Kip opened an issue of *Cover* to read the following news item:

MINA, recently cured of her drug addiction, this week releases what has been variously described as her 'Christian', 'Gospel', and 'Born Again' album. In addition, she has confirmed that she will be appearing at the Good News Rock Festival in Bletchley, Staffordshire on May 30th.

Wasting no time, he called the *Cover* office and asked to speak to Joe Grout, who had recently been appointed the paper's new editor.

'I'm not convinced the readers are going to be that

interested in the new Mina,' Grout said delicately after Kip
had proposed that he interview her.

Kip begged to disagree. 'People might find this whole
road-to-Damascus thing hard to believe,' he said, 'but for
that very reason I think they want to know more.'

'Maybe.'

'I really think so, Joe.'

'But I don't want anything major on this. Just a short
piece.'

'Sure. Whatever.'

'Eight hundred words.'

'You've got it.'

Surely Mina wouldn't refuse to see him now.

Cover, April 30th, 1983

MINA
A Saving Grace (Rebirth)

Dear God,
I suppose we should all be very happy that
Mina has stopped doing those terrible things
to herself. No one enjoys seeing such a lovely
girl go to pot (so to speak).

Trouble is, religion has never exactly been
conducive to creativity in the performing arts.
Well, not today, anyway. Maybe if Mina was
painting frescoes in the fourteenth century it
might be different, but she's not. She's making
pop records in the late twentieth century, and
anyone familiar with the works of Thy humble
servant Saint Cliff will know that God and pop
don't mix too fruitfully.

Oh sure, some of us are hip to The Five Blind Boys of Mississippi (or even Alabama), and that's all well and good. Bit of gospel never did anyone any harm. But our Mina wasn't born in Mississippi (or even Alabama), and she ain't exactly a tongue-speaking holy roller.

Mighty Father, I'll get to the point. When it comes to Mina (and the Velvets, the Stooges, et al.), the devil really does have all the best riffs. There, I've said it, and you may now strike me down. You will argue that no less a man than Bob Dylan has seen the light and recorded three whole platters in praise of your good self. I will counter that *Slow Train Coming*, *Saved* and *Shot Of Love* collectively aren't worth five minutes of *Blonde on Blonde* or *Blood on the Tracks*.

You don't have to be a paid-up Satanist to sense instinctively that *A Saving Grace* is an unwise career move. The cover alone is worrying enough. Whoever could have believed Mina *smiling* on an album sleeve? Then we get to the songs, which are as turgid and mealy mouthed as all Christian Rock is. I mean, really, after the heights scaled on *La Ronde* and the 'Consumed' EP, to sink to this seems pretty sad. There's even a song here called 'Morning Of Light', as if rebuffing the masterful reworking of that Nico song.

Written with one Darren Wade, who doubles on unremarkable lead guitar – Boris Salgado, where are you now? – these songs never rise above the most pedestrian kind of pop-rock. Tambourines are rattled, guitars strummed for Jesus, and Mina reins in the

vocal genius which made her singing so extraordinary. Doubtless, Lord, you'll be tapping
your foot to 'Gather' or 'Love And Only
Love', but most of us would rather swoon to
'Ghost' and 'The Death Of Desire'.

I'm sorry to be such a killjoy. I sincerely
wish I could be saved by Mina's new grace.
But if you could possibly see your way to
releasing her from the grip of born-again Chris-
tianity for just, say, a couple more albums, I
and many others would be eternally grateful.

Yours, genuflecting,

Don Barstow

19

Kip read Don Barstow's review with mounting indignation. Whatever the merits or otherwise of *A Saving Grace*, this churlish dismissal might well scupper any chance of Kip's interviewing Mina. He was tempted to write a kind of 'reply' for *Cover*, something along the lines of 'Beyond The Dead Zone: Mina's Journey Of Hope' . . .

He finally summoned the courage to call *Cover*.

'You calling about Mina, by any chance?' asked Joe Grout.

'I am, actually.'

'Well, look, there's some rather bad news on that front.'

'Really?' Kip felt as if someone had just punched him in the solar plexus.

'We've had a call from this Christian management company who claim to represent her, and what it comes down to is that she doesn't want you to interview her.'

Kip was dumbstruck.

'Kip?'

'I –'

'Any reason why she wouldn't talk to you?'

'Uh . . . no reason . . .'

'Well, look, I'm sorry . . .'

'Will she talk to anyone else from *Cover*?'

'Um . . . in principle, yes.'

'Who? Not Don.'

'Not Don.'

There was a brief silence.

'Kip, I have to go now. Any other ideas, don't hesitate to call. And sorry about all this again.'

'Right.'

For a while Kip couldn't move.

The next day, Kip went into Exeter to find a copy of *A Saving Grace*. On the bus back to Biddington, he listened to side one on his Walkman. It was strangely consoling to have her voice between his ears again. On 'Gather', she sounded like Sandy Denny crossed with Stevie Nicks. The decadent despair of *La Ronde* had completely gone.

By the time he was home, listening to 'Morning Of Light' at the beginning of side two, Kip was ready to pronounce the album a masterwork. What did Don Barstow, champion of Cabaret Voltaire, know? What did anyone at *Cover* know about the suffering one had to have endured to write 'Suicide Of The Soul'?

In the evening, Kip walked Winnie down to the river and up past Ilaston Wood. *A Saving Grace* played on his Walkman as he trudged through the marshy fields. Occasionally he stopped, realising Winnie was lagging behind.

Back at home, a note on the kitchen table informed him that his parents had gone into Exeter to a recital at the University. To Kip's relief, Gemma was nowhere to be seen.

The sun had gone down by the time Kip was sitting in his father's study with a large tumbler of whisky. He was smiling and singing softly to himself when he reached down to the bottom-right-hand drawer of Michael Wilson's desk and felt for the old army revolver his father kept in a wooden box for the day some Broadmoor escapee broke into the house.

Kip pulled the gun out of the drawer and placed it in his lap. Throwing back the last of the whisky, he began to dance slowly around the room, waving the gun around him, lost in the sound that filled his head – the sound of the Sacred Monsters Of Desire, and Mina screaming 'Art Of Darkness' . . .

20

Wandering through the grounds of Bletchley Priory, Kip wondered if it was going to rain. Wondered, too, if any of Mina's original fans had come to see her at the Good News Rock Festival. Looking around, he saw only smiling men in sandals, women in flowery blouses.

It occurred to him that he might be able to get backstage, but the whole concept of 'backstage' seemed a little incongruous at a Christian rock festival. He walked about, confirming to himself that the security operation was hardly on a military scale. Even the bouncers, if bounce they did, looked beatific.

'You wouldn't happen to know if Mina's around, would you?' he asked a security guard.

'Couldn't say, I'm afraid,' the man smiled.

'No matter. Just wanted her autograph.'

'I could try and get it for you.'

'You serious?'

'No problem.'

'That's really kind.' He thought for a second. 'Could you ask her to make it out to Kip?'

'Kip.'

'Yes.'

'Sure thing.'

Five minutes passed before the man returned. Looking slightly perplexed, he handed the programme back. 'Yours in Christ, Mina' read the autograph.

'D'you know her or something?' asked the guard.

'Why?'

'Cos she went a bit funny when I said your name.'

'Yeah?'

'Yeah.'

Kip could hear an announcement for a gospel choir over the PA, followed by the choir itself. The white crowd was singing along to 'Oh, Happy Day'. Perhaps Mina was singing, too.

It was a little after 6 o'clock when he positioned himself in front of the stage. He watched three portly roadies set up the stage for Mina's set.

His heart began to beat fast. The crowd were filing back in, and the evening air was cooling.

At 6.30 the roadies left the stage and a beaming Christian DJ wandered up to the microphone. He was from Radio Joy, 'your Good News station', and he wanted to introduce 'a very special young lady'.

'When I tell you that this girl has been down to the depths and risen back up, I know you'll understand why we're so pleased to have her with us today. If anyone can witness to the miracle of the Lord's power, ladies and gentlemen, she can. So would you put your hands together and give a huge Good News welcome to . . . *Mina*!'

As the cheers filled the air, Kip saw Mina for the first time in almost a year. She looked radiant, an angelic vision in a long white dress. Her honey-golden hair, restored to its original length, was tied back in a pony tail. The smiling face glowed with health.

'Praise Jesus,' she said.

It was the curly-haired Darren Wade who counted the band in, and Kip quickly recognised one of the songs from *A Saving Grace*.

As Mina's voice pierced through the muddy sound, Kip gazed up at her, enraptured. 'Oh gather here, one and all,' she sang, 'gather as we break the fall . . .'

When the song had ended, Mina took the microphone out of its stand to introduce the second number. 'I used to sing about the evening of light,' she said. 'Now I sing of the morning.'

Kip felt for his father's revolver and drew it slowly from his duffle bag. He took aim from twenty yards and fired two explosive shots into Mina's torso. All around him people dropped to the ground as she staggered back and fell against the drum kit. He saw the white dress turn red.

Among the men who eventually ran up to him was the security guard who'd obtained Mina's autograph backstage. All the colour had drained from the man's face. Kip could hear the sound of screaming from every direction. Everything was very distant, as if he was looking down the wrong end of a telescope.

He said nothing and stared straight ahead at the stage.

Crestview House,
5th Jan., 1995

Dear Stevie

Not the best of days, and now it's pouring. Didn't get all my pills – Dr Spassky said there'd been some mistake. Nothing good on telly, so I've just re-read *NME* and re-listened to the Silver Jews album you sent me.

Trouble is, the older I get the more violent I seem to

like my music. I'm still playing the Pantera album, and
Ministry. Have become a right old headbanger, which
is fine with Spassky provided I'm not banging aforesaid
head against wall. Sometimes I walk around all day
with Metallica's 'Sad But True' in my head. Sad but
true . . .

I guess it's hardly surprising no one wants me to write
for them. Personally, I think I could write a great column
– call it 'Meditations From The Nut Ward' – but I guess
they don't see it that way. In any case, ever since *Cover* bit
the dust I don't exactly have 'contacts' in the music
press . . .

The increasingly cyclical nature of music is becoming
tiresome in the extreme. Now I gather everything I
loathed so much in the early eighties – all that horrid
Depeche synth-pop – is coming back with a vengeance.
On the basis of all this, one can make pretty accurate
predictions of what's coming over the horizon: rockabilly,
deconstructed white funk, espresso-bar soul, shambling
anorak bands. Revivals of revivals, no less. It's probably
about time we started calling rock 'pop' again. Oooh the
Zeitgeist, doncha just love it!

Do you ever hear from Ava Cadaver – or Mrs Janovitz
as we must now refer to her? I can't believe she went back
to Yonkers after all that time. Still, at least she didn't
marry a Goth.

I don't think my family really like to see me here, and
who can blame them? Mum still feels like it's her fault I'm
here at all. They're due to come on Sunday, though I dare
say my father will find some excuse not to be present. I
haven't seen Gemma since she began campaigning for the
ordination of women priests.

Glad to hear your record label's flourishing. Pity I can't

review any of your releases, eh? Hope you're keeping that virus at bay. Any chance of a visit?

Lotsa luv,

Kip.

P.S.   I'm reading John Oldfield's book at the moment. Hard going but brilliant, of course. On page 257 there's a reference to 'the peculiar aptness of Mina's death' and a mention of yours truly. Fame at last! I showed it to Spassky and he smiled.

Founded in 1986, Serpent's Tail publishes the innovative and the challenging.

If you would like to receive a catalogue of our current publications please write to:

FREEPOST
Serpent's Tail
4 Blackstock Mews
LONDON N4 2BR

(No stamp necessary if your letter is posted in the United Kingdom.)